# Burrangong Creek

The outskirts to the east of Wagga were flat, featureless industrial estates; invariably concrete yards containing colourbond buildings in various colours with bright signwriting, surrounded by chainlink fencing. Nate turned his old Mazda three through one particular pair of open chainlink gates, to park next to one particular pale green colourbond building. He took his bag to the front of his van, before going inside that building to clock-on and make a mug of coffee in the kitchen. Although early, just past dawn, Nationwide Couriers in Wagga Wagga was stirring as more and more cars arrived, and more and more courier drivers made tea and coffee. Smalltalk about cricket being summer, football next season, and bushfires burning in the north of the state. Most of Australia was parched and dry and sure to be a bad fire season, although the country around Wagga was a sparsely treed plain of grass and less of a fire risk.

The momentary snarl of a compression brake shattered early morning quiet, and again and again. Then a squeal of brakes as the bellow of a diesel engine exhaust was now clearly audible. Unwashed mugs were put away before they trooped to meet the semi from Sydney with that day's parcels, now backed to the big doors of the shed. As always for a Monday, Nate put himself last in the queue to ease close to Dave peering into the spare wheel well of the semi-trailer.

"G'day mate," Nate greeted.

1

"G'day Nate," Dave replied. "These are for you," as Dave handed three bulky envelopes across.

Nate now held envelopes more valuable than the legitimate load that morning.

"Does your run cover Young?" Dave asked.

"Yeah mate." Nate knew it like the back of his hand: the suburbs north of Wagga first, then Junee, Cootamundra, Young, Cowra, Boorowa, Harden, Gundagai, and back to Wagga, as well as smaller towns near those bigger centres.

"Jack Bishop is moving to Young this week."

"I pity him."

"Trev reckons there's potential there."

"I'd say Trev's right."

One of the envelopes in Nate's hand was for Jack Bishop, now living just off Colin Knott Drive.

"They call these the Ice Highways," Dave said.

"More than ice, isn't it?" Nate replied.

"Dunno. I'm just the driver.

"And I'm just the deliverer."

Nate took those envelopes to van number three, his van, where he opened the front passenger door to place them in his bag alongside a plastic container with sandwiches, a thermos of coffee and a plastic bottle of water. Nate zipped his bag closed, slammed the door of his van, before heading to the back of the semi-trailer to stack pre-sorted parcels onto a trolley brought out by guys who worked mornings only.

2

Nate wheeled the trolley to the back of his van, where he kind-of placed and kind-of threw those parcels inside. Nate then wheeled the now empty trolley to the partitioned office inside the shed, where Jacko gave Nate a clipboard with his manifest, and the barcode scanner already programmed. Nate scrolled addresses on the manifest while he planned his run in his head. He had a diversion to Old Junee and another to Binalong, which weren't a problem.

"See ya Jacko." Nate offered.

I0556508

"See ya Nate."

Nate strolled to his van, climbed up, placed the clipboard and scanner on the passenger seat, buckled up, started up and waited for another van to cross his path. This week's drug run included envelopes for Aidan at Estella, Justin at Brucedale and Jack at Harefield. Next week Jack would be at Young, whatever address. Nate decided to talk with Jack to find that out. With the yard now clear Nate pulled out to head off. Mondays were quiet for deliveries, being parcels lodged Saturday and Sunday in Sydney, so those drug drop-offs were easy to fit in. The sky was much lighter as Nate headed west towards northern Wagga and the first of his deliveries.

# Burrangong Creek

by

## Mark Morey

*All rights reserved*

Names, characters and incidents depicted in this book are products of the author's imagination or are used fictitiously. Any resemblance to actual events, locales, organisations, or persons, living or dead, is entirely coincidental and beyond the intent of the author.

No part of this book may be reproduced or transmitted in any form or by any means, electronic or mechanical, including photocopying, recording, or by any information storage and retrieval system, without permission in writing from the author

Mark Morey

http://markmorey.blogspot.com

Copyright ©

978-0-6487869-6-2

Published In Australia

January 2021

4

## Other Works by Mark Morey

The Red Sun will Come - June 2012

Souls in Darkness - August 2012

The Governess and the Stalker - July 2014

Maidens in the Night - September 2014

One Hundred Days - September 2015

The Last Great Race – April 2016

The Adulterous Bride – October 2016

No Darkness – March 2017

In Our Memories – November 2017

Blood Never Sleeps – March 2018

Ketsumeidan – October 2018

Yuejin – Aim High! – July 2019

Wenge – Destroy The Old! – July 2019

Ice – February 2020

Across the Border – July 2020

- Akubra hat – a broad-brimmed hat often worn in rural parts of Australia, made from the felt of rabbit fur.

- Australia (The Commonwealth of Australia). Founded on 1 January, 1901, after referendums in each colony of Australia saw a majority vote in favour of the proposed Australian constitution. After federation, each former colony became a state within the Commonwealth of Australia, retaining control of day to day government activities such as transport, healthcare, education, police and law and order. The sixth-largest country in the world, Australia is the oldest, flattest and driest inhabited continent, with the least fertile soils. This dryness and lack of soil fertility is why Australia has a population of only 26 million, with most of this population concentrated within a well-watered and fertile strip of land between the Great Dividing Range and the sea. Inland Australia is dry, flat and magnificently, endlessly spacious.

- Base – methamphetamine (also known as ice)

- Burrangong – means 'meeting place of kangaroos by the water' in the Wiradjuri language. The first European in this area of New South Wales was James White who established Burrangong Station in 1826.

- CCO – Community Corrections Order. This may include mandatory minimum community work hours, curfews, and rehabilitation treatment where this is deemed appropriate.

- Centrelink – the Australian Commonwealth Government social security agency

- China girl – heroin

- Cowra. A small city of 10,063, by car 70 kilometres north of Young.

- Coke – cocaine

- Doing lines – snorting cocaine

- Ecky – MDMA (also known as Ecstasy or E)

- Escort – the Australian sex industry is regulated at a state level where New South Wales decriminalised their sex industry many decades ago. It is possible to work from home, do outcalls, and that's all legal.

- Leeton. A town of 8,623 purpose-designed and built to support the Murrumbidgee Irrigation Area in the Riverina region of New South Wales.

- New South Wales. The colony of New South Wales was first settled in 1789 as a convict settlement on Sydney Cove, later to become the state of New South Wales within the Commonwealth of Australia. New South Wales extends from a relatively narrow strip of fertile and well-watered land on the coastal side of the Great Dividing Range, to fertile but less well-watered agricultural land west of this mountain range, including the South-West Slopes region in the western foothills of the Great Dividing Range. Further west in New South Wales the quality of soil deteriorates to semi-desert, and to desert in the far west. Rainfall is variable in inland New South Wales with drought never far away. Water is a precious commodity in most of inland Australia, and in most of inland New South Wales. As result farms are large, while inland towns and cities are small and sparsely spread. The New South Wales school year runs from late summer to early the next summer (late January to early December).

- Newstart – the Australian unemployment benefit (currently A$277.85 a week or A$179.15 below the Australian poverty line).

- Orange. A sizeable and growing city in the Central West region of New South Wales. By car, Orange is 160 kilometres north-east of Young, not far by Australian standards, with a population of 40,493. Known for fruit orchards, wineries, and occasional heavy winter snowfalls.

- TAFE – Technical and Further Education. Originally tertiary educational institutions operated by Australian state governments training tradespeople through apprenticeships. In more recent times TAFEs have concentrated on a broad range of tertiary vocational education qualifications, which may take anything from several months to a year to complete, or longer if part-time.

- Thong – a backless sandal (called a flip-flop in the USA). What Americans call thongs, Australians call g-strings.

- Ute – utility (cab and tray vehicle)

- Young. Originally settled in 1861 and located in the South-West Slopes region of New South Wales, Young has a population of 7,170 (2016), and is relatively poor with a median adult income of A$34,528 (2016). Employment in Young revolves around supporting the surrounding agricultural district, consisting of broad acre farms grazing livestock for meat, cherry orchards and some wineries. Young has a small tourism industry with wineries and cherry orchards being features. Young's climate features hot, dry summers and cool, moist winters; sometimes cold enough for light snowfalls. Young's public transport routes connect it to Orange and further to Sydney (370 kilometres).

- Youth Allowance – a social security benefit for young students or apprentices, subject to means testing

- Wagga Wagga - means 'dancing and celebration' in the Wiradjuri language. Wagga Wagga is commonly known as 'Wagga'. A relatively prosperous inland city in the Riverina region of New South Wales, with a population of 56,442. By car, Wagga is 120 kilometres south-west of Young.

- Weed – cannabis

## Chapter One

Josh heard Lisa shouting at Tracy and Mia well before he reached Daniel's house. He paused, not wanting to intrude. But Josh was a customer and Lisa spent half her day screeching at their two daughters anyway. Josh walked on where, parked in the driveway, was Daniel's new SUV: a black BMW X5. Brand new and not second-hand but new to Daniel. Josh walked past the BMW to a back yard scattered with toys: a plastic tricycle, a plastic toy pram and plastic dolls, beyond which was a colour-coordinated Weldmesh fence separating a paved area and swimming pool. Daniel's block of land sloped from front to rear, which allowed a lower level at the back of his house where deals were done. At the door Josh pressed the buzzer while hearing Daniel trying to bring order to the commotion inside. Apparently Mia had Tracy's doll which was a major problem, despite three or four dolls abandoned in a yard of lush lawn, shrubs in enclosures of tanbark fenced by redgum sleepers, and a rotary clothes hoist. Josh heard heavy footsteps before the door opened.

"Ah Josh," Daniel greeted. "The usual?"

"Yes thanks," Josh replied.

Daniel was gone for just a moment, before he returned with a small, ziplock plastic bag. Josh reached into his back pocket for his wallet where he took out a fifty dollar note.

They exchanged money for goods before Josh put his wallet and the bag in his back pocket.

"See you next time," Daniel said.

"Yeah, sure," Josh replied. Unlike some in Young, Josh was casual; he didn't buy anywhere near enough to pay for that BMW parked where it was to show off to neighbours. Josh headed to the street strangely aware of somebody watching him. He stopped to look but nobody was there. Josh continued with that same, odd feeling. He put his head down; maybe police had Daniel under surveillance. Josh was sure there was someone, but that street was quiet and even Lisa had stopped screaming. Josh walked past brick veneer houses where nothing moved, around the corner to the next intersection where he headed right to yet another brick veneer house. From the street Josh heard another household of commotion: Kev and his mother were at it again. Kev bellowed Mum was a lazy slut while Mum shouted he was just a loser, plus a few adjectives. In a yard of dead grass and weeds, the shouting and swearing was clear through the open, living room window before something smashed inside.

"Fuck!" Kev swore.

Mum must have thrown something at Kev, as was her way. Josh walked beside their rented house to where his bedroom window was open. He reached up to peel away the flyscreen before taking a big breath for the effort to hoist himself up to the windowsill. There he dropped down to a

11

floor of polished boards and a rug. His room for the past few years since Dad cleared out. Beyond his bedroom the argument continued as Josh grabbed his backpack. In it he stuffed underwear, socks, a few shirts, his trousers for work, and DOOM Eternal. That would do as Josh sat on the windowsill once more, before dropping his backpack to the ground and lowering himself to follow. He went to his car, not a shining black BMW but a faded red, 1999 Commodore. Josh stopped; still certain he was being watched. He looked around but still saw nobody. Josh took the remote to unlock his car; tossed his backpack onto the passenger seat before climbing in and buckling up. There he started the engine, reversed out and headed away.

It wasn't far to where James lived with his family. Josh could have walked but he needed his car. As always the back door was unlocked, as Josh let himself in to knock on James' bedroom door.

"G'day Josh," James greeted.

"G'day James," Josh replied. "Mind if I crash here for a while?"

"Sure, no problem."

James didn't ask why because he didn't need to.

"I brought DOOM Eternal," Josh said.

"Great! We can continue from last time."

James cleared clothes strewn across the floor of his room while Josh reached into his backpack for the game. In a moment they were side-by-side and cross-legged on the floor, engrossed in the next stage of their battle.

* * *

Sophie checked the backdoor which was unlocked. As soon as she entered the kitchen, she heard the flop of Jack's thongs.

"How did it go?" Jack asked from the doorway.

Sophie went to the fridge for a bottle of orange cordial and the jug of cold water. She poured a drink while knowing Jack was dying to know. She sipped from her glass already wet with condensation before putting the cordial and water away.

Sophie leaned against the counter. "I saw a few," she said.

"And...?"

"One's promising. I'm certain he's casual. I followed him home, it wasn't far, but there was a fight."

"What sort of fight?"

"People in the house. He got his things and left in his car. I jogged behind and it wasn't far."

Jack rubbed his chin while Mum came into the room.

"Sophie saw someone promising," Jack said.

"Good," Mum said. "What now?"

"Sophie; you can show me where this guy is."

"I can".

"You better be right about this shithole," Mum said.

"Young is a shithole," Jack said, "but there are only two dealers. For sure this will work."

"Are you sure Sophie is right to do this?"

"I need a local contact and someone younger will be better. Sophie's sensible, she even samples as you know."

"Yeah, alright," Jessica grumbled.

"I'm fine Mum," Sophie said. More than finding a young contact for Jack, Sophie hoped she would find a friend, if not more than just a friend.

"Sophie...?" Jack asked.

Sophie finished her drink. "Come with me Jack."

Sophie led the way to the garage where Jack's pride and joy, a Valiant Charger E49 in bright orange, was parked away from the sun. If being discreet while keeping a potential contact under surveillance was their aim, then a racing car from the 1970s was not the way to do that. Sophie waited for Jack to unlock his car before she slid into a vinyl bucket seat from many decades past while smiling brightly. Men and their cars.

* * *

Chloe glanced at the clock on the wall, after four, just as she heard footsteps. She looked up to see Matthew Wall, Matt, a semi-regular. A methamphetamine addict showing the signs: haggard and drawn from losing weight, pimples and acne, scabby lips; a few missing teeth. It wasn't that methamphetamine, ice, did that, but heavy users neglected

14

personal hygiene and almost everything else in their lives, so consumed were they for their next hit.

"Hi Chloe," Matt greeted.

"Hi Matt," Chloe replied. "Take a seat." Matt sat on the couch beside Chloe's messy desk. Chloe sat beside. "What can I do for you or is it the same?"

"It's the same."

Always the same. "What about the strategies we talked about?"

"Making new friends and playing games with my friends. Well, that helps to fill in the day, but not enough."

"How about a job?"

"I'm not ready for a job yet."

"Are you still craving?"

He nodded his head. "Yeah, too much. But now it's hard – too hard. Mum threw me out for stealing from her purse and selling her watch. I got no money but I'm awful bad."

"How you feel now will pass in time."

"I really need a loan, you know. Just fifty and I'll pay you back next week."

Chloe knew what that was about. "Sorry Matt," she said.

"You can't help me then?" Matt asked while studying stained green carpet.

"No I can't," Chloe said while contemplating her carpet too. "I can help you get your life in order, help you find a job when you want that, but I won't lend you money for drugs."

"I understand," Matt mumbled while still studying the floor.

"Are you on the waiting list for rehab?"

"Me and a hundred others."

Chloe sighed: If only there was a decent rehab system.

"You've still got the pamphlet I gave you?" Chloe asked.

"I tried that but it didn't work for me," Matt said.

Chloe wasn't surprised. "How you feel now will pass," she said.

"I know."

"No bad thoughts?" Chloe then asked.

"It's just I need a fix."

"Hang in there, Matt."

"Yeah, thanks."

Matt left, no doubt to pester someone else for a loan that would never be repaid while Chloe wished she could do more. But she was only a counsellor where people like Matt needed expert assistance until they eventually overcame their urges. Even then they might relapse, Matt almost certainly would, but only live-in, full-time treatment had a chance of success. It was almost four-thirty so Chloe turned the sign in the door, locked that door behind her, and walked to her car baking in the sun. Soon she was on her way, airconditioning blasting, while still thinking about Matt and many others. But all Chloe could do was plug the cracks or whatever that saying was, and maybe even have small victories from time to time.

Young, New South Wales, was a typical, dysfunctional, larger inland town. As dysfunctional as Young was, the main shopping streets, broad Boorowa Street and the parallel Lovell Street, were truly delightful. Running east to west and splitting the town virtually in two, they contained countless examples of early 20th Century Federation-style buildings still in use as food retailers, clothing retailers, banks, hardware stores, hairdressers, restaurants, cafes, takeaways, Headspace of course, and everything to be expected for a sizeable town supporting smaller towns and farmers in the nearby vicinity. Young, like the South-West-Slopes Region of New South Wales, was on gently undulating land, with inner areas containing many examples of older Federation-style houses, mostly in weatherboard. Further away from the town centre, later 20th Century developments were less aesthetically pleasing, being either charmless brick veneer houses, always in orange-cream coloured brick with terracotta tiled roofs, or cheap 'fibro' houses built of cement sheeting with the vertical gaps between sheets covered by wooden battens, and always topped by corrugated iron roofs invariably needing a repaint. There were some new suburban developments in Young, surprisingly with quite a few McMansions, while the outskirts had multi-hectare blocks with multi-million dollar genuine

17

mansions for the wealthy, business-owning aristocracy of the area.

Chloe reached her home: a spacious, early 20th Century Federation-style weatherboard house under renovation. For all its faults, Young was an affordable place rent or buy your own home, where bigger cities in Australia were not, and that was another problem for the youth of Young. Even though job opportunities were limited, it was an affordable place to live and they had their support networks. Chloe parked her Toyota Corolla in the carport noting that Luke wasn't yet home, to step into bright sunshine and heat. In the hills at an altitude Young wasn't as hot as further inland, although more than hot enough on that sunny December day. Inside their house was warm but pleasant, except for sawdust and the smell of paint. Chloe dumped her handbag in their bedroom, where the smell of paint was the strongest and she had to mind the ladder. She went to the kitchen, now with solid timber cupboards and granite bench tops, to open the fridge, grab the bottle of white wine from the evening before, and pour a glass. Chloe sat on a stool sipping her cool, refreshing drink while hearing Luke's footsteps in the background. He kissed her cheek.

"Do you want a glass of wine?" Chloe asked.

"I'll have a beer," Luke said.

He grabbed a stubby, twisted the top with the usual hiss, and drank some before sitting beside Chloe.

"How was your day?" Luke asked.

"The usual. Youth self-harm and suicide isn't so much of a problem here, for reasons I don't understand, but drug addiction is. Not surprising. Not enough jobs, and what jobs there are, are casual part-time or gig contractors."

"Like everywhere else."

"I think that's why they stay here. They have friends for support here, while if they moved they wouldn't necessarily be better off." Chloe sipped her wine while thinking. "Are drugs a problem, beyond what I see at work?"

Luke blew his cheeks out. "We suspect a couple of dealers but to investigate them would be pointless. If there are other dealers beyond those we suspect, they'll fill the vacuum as if nothing happened, and if there aren't then new dealers will move in and take over."

"Or users will go to Cowra up the road."

"Yeah."

"The real solution is to give youth something productive to do, like full-time jobs. But with high unemployment and higher underemployment, drug use is inevitable."

"For sure."

"I know this is radical and even goes against the United Nations, not that Australia is beholden to the rulings of that body, but if we controlled and regulated drugs we can solve many problems. For a start we can divert money currently spent on trying to eliminate drugs to rehabilitation."

"And put me out of a job?"

Chloe smiled. "There are many other crimes for Senior Constable Luke Scott to investigate, I'm sure. After all, you're letting drug dealers slip under the radar."

"The most destructive drug is alcohol. Most domestic violence is alcohol related, as are other crimes of a violent nature."

"Is there much crime from drug users?"

Luke frowned. "Not really. Some break and enters and some motor vehicle theft, but we're well below state averages on those two. Stealing from retail stores is up but not dramatically so. When we catch perpetrators they usually get a suspended sentence, but they should be sent to drug rehab except there aren't enough places."

"And have job opportunities once they're clean, so they don't relapse out of boredom."

"Yeah."

Chloe finished her wine. "Well Luke, what would you like for dinner?"

"Anything that's not too much bother."

Chloe liked that about her husband; he was low-maintenance and easygoing. "I have some frozen hake fillets and some frozen chips, with a fresh salad and white wine."

"Sounds good."

Chloe headed to the laundry to raid their freezer for what was sure to be a decent dinner after a long and even frustrating day. It was good to be home and not plugging the cracks or whatever that saying was, because the problems of Young, like the problems of New South Wales, like the problems of Australia, like the problems of the Western world, were beyond one counsellor at Headspace. All she could do was get the odd victory or two while hoping the bigger issue, the lack of decent jobs for younger millennials, would resolve in time.

## Chapter Two

Josh checked tags of gardening tools, matching them to bin labels and moving those in wrong places. It was surprising that so many were out of order. Customers must pull them out, check them, and put them back anywhere. He kept at it: shovels, spades, picks, mattocks, rakes. They had two or three brands of everything.

"Excuse me?" a sweet, female voice asked.

Josh turned to face a beautiful teen girl: tall, slender, fair, blonde hair to her waist, gorgeous blue-grey eyes, and dressed in a burgundy halter top tight across her bust and the tiniest of denim shorts. Shorts which suited her given she was slim but feminine, especially with long, slender legs. Then Josh was aware he was staring.

"Can I help you?" he asked.

"I'm looking for a rake."

"What sort of rake? For raking dirt and stones or for raking leaves from grass?"

"Raking leaves from grass."

Josh had to get close to this girl to reach for the rakes. "These plastic rakes are for raking leaves: one is 9 99 and the other 15 99, but often you get what you pay for." Josh pulled one out. "This one is more expensive, but it will last longer so is better value."

She took the rake from Josh to contemplate it with a frown. "I'll take this one."

"Good. My name's Josh."

She laughed. "I see that, Josh."

His name tag on his overalls.

"I'm Sophie Weaver and I'm new here from Wagga."

"Young will be quiet for you after Wagga," Josh said.

"What do people do here?"

Josh thought. "Hang out with friends, play games, meet at the gardens by Burrangong Creek, go to the Chinese Gardens just out of town, go to the Southern Cross Cinema when its open, and I have this job a couple of days a week."

"Selling at the local Mitre 10."

"Yeah. I'll take you to the cash register."

Josh headed through the quiet hardware store with Sophie by his side.

"Do you play games, Josh?" Sophie asked.

"Sometimes."

"Do you want to come to my house one day to play games? It's just I'm new here and I don't have friends yet."

Josh couldn't believe that. "Yeah, sure, anytime."

"This afternoon?"

"I finish at five."

"Five is good."

They reached the register.

"How are you paying?" Josh asked.

Sophie struggled with a front pocket of her tight shorts to extract a 20 dollar note. She handed it across. Josh scanned the barcode, entered 20 dollars for the register to prompt four dollars change, which Josh grabbed from the drawer. He gave the two coins and the receipt to Sophie who once more had to struggle with her front pocket.

"Do you have a pen and paper?" Sophie asked.

Josh grabbed a stocktake pad and a pencil from the shelf beneath the register to place them on the counter. Sophie wrote on the back of one page with her tongue sticking out, before tearing the sheet and handing it to Josh. He read: 37 Blackett Avenue, Young.

"I'll see you just after five, Sophie."

"Thank you for the rake."

Sophie turned to leave while Josh admired her from behind. She had the most gorgeous figure he'd ever seen. He wondered how old: 16 or 17 maybe.

"Josh...?" John's voice broke into Josh's thoughts.

"Sorry," Josh said. "Just sold a rake."

"To her?"

"New in town."

"Nice."

Josh didn't say anything but mentally agreed. Nice didn't begin to describe Sophie Weaver; she brightened Young simply by being there.

\* \* \*

Blackett Avenue was in a poorer part of Young, although most of Young wasn't particularly well off. But Blackett

24

Avenue was poorer while number 37 was a typical rental house: older in fibro, painted white with dark brown window frames, and a corrugated iron roof that had seen better days. The sort of rental house that Josh might have lived in except his grandfather knew a real estate agent. Josh climbed cracked, concrete steps that led to an uneven concrete path which took him to more concrete steps to the front porch. There, Josh used a tarnished, brass knocker on an aged but freshly painted front door. Moments later Sophie opened it; delicious in her barely-there clothes.

"Hi Josh."

"Hi Sophie."

"Come in."

It was hot inside where a passage split that house in two, as was typical of older houses. Sophie led the way to a living room painted fawn with polished boards and a standalone gas heater in front of a boarded-up fireplace. A smallish television on a small table and a lounge suite in green corduroy looked lonely together in that room.

"I won't be long," Sophie said.

Moments later she reappeared with a late 40s man grey at his temples, and a woman some years younger.

"Josh, this is my mother Jessica, and Jack."

"Hi," Josh greeted, while Jack put his hand out for Josh to shake, to which Josh responded. Clearly Jack was Sophie's stepfather. Jessica was Sophie some years older: similar height or tall for a woman, a little fuller in her figure while still slim; the same blue-grey eyes and the same blonde hair, although part-way down her back rather than almost to her waist. Even dressed in a similar, body-revealing style, with a tight blue t-shirt and jeans tight to almost be a second skin. Jack had a tanned face and nice smile lines around his eyes. He wore a black t-shirt with a car logo, something about a Valiant Charger, knee-length khaki shorts and thongs.

"It's good to see Sophie making friends," Jessica said.

"We met where I work."

"Even better," Jessica said as she lit a cigarette. She grabbed a tin ashtray from the former mantel of the former fireplace.

"We're going to play games," Sophie said.

"Have fun."

Josh followed Sophie to the corridor, which had a dining room to the right with a square laminate table and four dark blue plastic chairs, and a small kitchen at the end showing its age. Sophie's room was opposite the dining room: decently-sized with a single bed pushed against the wall, a bedside cabinet with a smartphone and purse on top, a freestanding clear varnished plywood wardrobe, and a metal and laminate stand with a small television on top, a Playstation 4 standing beside, and controllers and games in two wire baskets beneath. Unmarked beige walls and dark blue carpet, with a view of a paling fence.

"Which game?" Sophie asked. "DOOM Eternal?"

"I'm playing that at the moment," Josh said.

"Ah. Call of Duty: Modern Warfare?"

"Yeah, that's good."

Sophie got that ready including the controllers which she draped to the bed a few metres away.

"We can sit here," Sophie said as she sat on the pink quilt cover, next to a big teddy bear with a pink bow. Josh sat beside feeling somewhat awkward. Her room, her bed, and she was the most beautiful girl Josh had ever seen. He wanted to do more than play Call of Duty: Modern Warfare, he tingled even, but he'd just met Sophie while Jack and Jessica were just beyond a closed, white-painted door. So Call of Duty: Modern Warfare it was and hopefully his tingles would abate.

"I'm being a bad host," Sophie said. "Do you want something to drink?"

"Yes please."

"I have Schweppes orange cordial, either with cold water from the fridge or soda water. Which one?"

"Cold water will be fine."

Sophie took a moment to get glasses each, which were placed on the floor beside respective pairs of feet. Part-way into their first mission Josh realised Sophie was a gamer girl and then some, which probably was why she invited Josh to play, given girls weren't so much into this type of game. But certainly Sophie was a gamer girl, and in the short time he'd been there, sociable too. As they played Josh suspected that his evening might be more than just playing games. He wouldn't be surprised if Jack and Jessica invited Josh to stay for dinner, as Sophie's friend. Josh smiled to himself at that thought.

Sophie played well; more of an adversary than James and Josh's other friends. In fact she beat him quite thoroughly in that mission. Looking satisfied she put her controller on her bed.

"Beat you."

"I'll beat you next time."

"I'd like to see that. Do you want to stay for dinner? I can ask Mum."

*Did he?* "Yes please."

Sophie left the room with Josh once more admiring her cute bottom. Moments later: "Mum said that's fine. It's roast beef and there's plenty. It's almost ready."

Josh followed Sophie to the dining room laid out with a tablecloth, cutlery, and a stubby of beer.

"Drink?" Sophie asked.

"That cordial's fine." Josh didn't drink much alcohol and he didn't like beer.

Sophie grabbed their glasses from her room while Jack sat next to the stubby of beer.

"Good game?" Jack asked.

"Sophie won," Josh said.

"She usually does. Beer o'clock," Jack then said before twisting the top of the stubby to drink a mouthful. "Lived here long?" Jack asked.

"Our family goes back a long way. Not quite as far as the days of Lambing Flat, but a while."

Jack nodded his head thoughtfully. "We moved here for a business opportunity. Even though Young is smaller than Wagga, there's less competition here."

Josh nodded his head in understanding. There were many businesses in Wagga Wagga competing with each other.

"Later I'll show you my car," Jack said. "A Valiant Charger E49. A genuine one and not a lookalike."

Josh didn't have a clue what that was. "That'll be nice," he said.

Sophie laid out plates before Jessica brought a large plate of sliced roast beef still steaming, and Sophie returned with a bowl of sliced, baked potatoes and a bowl of green vegetables. That was placed on the small table along with tongs.

"Sophie said you work at a hardware store," Jessica said while Jack served.

"I work three days a week at Mitre 10. I'm looking for something with more hours but it's a start."

"Did you pass year 12?" Sophie asked.

"I did."

"I'm doing year 12 at Young High School, next year."

That made Sophie 16 or 17, as Josh guessed. "That's the same school I went to," Josh said.

"Is it good?"

"Yeah, it's good."

Jessica disappeared to the kitchen; she too had a nice figure from behind. She returned with a bowl of gravy. Their meal was fine and better than Mum who either cooked it half raw or dried it out.

"Do you have family here?" Jessica asked.

"My mother lives with her partner while Dad lives with his girlfriend and their child, who's my youngest sister. I have a twin brother, not identical, who lives in Sydney, and a younger sister still living with Mum. I'm staying with a friend."

"Sophie is our oldest, youngest and only."

For an only child Sophie wasn't spoiled but instead showed maturity. She was two or even three years younger than Josh but already he regarded her as a friend. He contemplated his gamer girl just a friend, who he wouldn't mind having as his real girlfriend when he got to know her better. Josh then realised something.

"Do you have your own business?" he asked.

"You can say that," Jessica said. "Yes, we do."

"And Young has opportunities for you?"

"Yes it does," Jack said.

That was good.  Meal was good too; especially Sophie's orange cordial.

"Do you want to play the next mission tomorrow?" Sophie asked.

"I'm working tomorrow so it'll have to be the same time."

"That's fine."

"You can stay for dinner again," Jessica said.

"Thank you."

This was a lovely family.  Their meal was rounded off with bowls of ice cream for dessert, which was nice on a warm day in a fibro house with a corrugated iron roof.  Hot inside in summer, and Josh knew from friends who lived in similar houses, freezing cold in winter.  That gas heater had better be good.

"That was a nice meal," Josh said.

"I'll show you my car," Jack said.

Sophie went with Jack and Sophie to the garage, also fibro with a corrugated iron roof, which held a big, orange car from some years past.  Shining bright like it was made yesterday, with many black stripes including a '4' etched into the vertical stripes on the sides.

"That's nice," Josh said.  "What's the four for?"

"That indicates a four speed gearbox.  The previous model had three speeds.  In the days when this was made, Bathurst was for unmodified production cars so manufacturers made special models to win."

31

"Did this model win?"

"It won a few races but Chrysler withdrew their works team, so private Charger entrants were up against works Holdens and works Fords. They came third and fourth at Bathurst in 1972."

"Ah. Looks nice though."

"Thanks."

Josh didn't really want to leave but he knew he shouldn't intrude on this family for too long.

"Thanks for the meal and showing me your car," Josh said to Jack, who shook his hand as farewell.

"I'll walk you to your car," Sophie said.

They walked along the drive to Josh's car where the evening was pleasant. More than pleasant – beautiful. Sophie stood really close on that quiet evening.

"Can I kiss you?" Josh asked.

"You can kiss me."

Josh put his hands around her slender waist to kiss her lips. Gorgeous in his arms.

"Beat you tomorrow, gamer girl."

"That'll be the day!"

Josh turned away to press the remote before getting into his car, while thinking that hug and kiss meant he had a girlfriend in all but name. He started up and drove away.

* * *

Sophie headed to the backdoor, barely believing her luck. Handsome: tall, lean, fresh skin, big doe-like brown eyes, full lips, and wavy, almost curly, black hair. More handsome than at Mitre 10 in his overalls. And really nice. And interested in her. She walked through the laundry to the kitchen where Mum washed plates.

"Are you sure he uses?" Jack asked from the doorway.

"He went to the back of Daniel Stewart's house for a few minutes," Sophie said.

"Did you invite him back?"

"I did."

"We can check that tomorrow."

Sophie wondered how Mum or Jack would check, but that wasn't her problem. Jack wanted Sophie to find someone so she did, and it seemed she now had a boyfriend. Better than other guys she'd met, better than Jason in Wagga. Young wasn't such a bad place after all. Aware she was smiling brightly, Sophie went to her room and closed her door. There she lay on her bed with her nipples tingling against her top and her pussy sparkling, throbbing even, and wet, so wet. Aching for attention. She loosened the button and the zip of her shorts and slid her hand inside her panties.

## Chapter Three

The traffic on Victoria Road never stopped. The endless roar of car tyres, the odd loud car exhaust, trucks bellowing, every now and then a siren; it was terrible. Glen leaned against the counter as the buzzer for pump seven rang. He looked across the forecourt to a motorcycle rider in black leather, so pressed the button for that pump. In the office Charan worked noiselessly while Glen's contemplation of the din of passing traffic was interrupted by the motorcycle rider paying 15 17 using a Visa debit card and not wanting a receipt, as was normal. Glen then thought about the endless traffic noise of Sydney again. Where he came from had no opportunities, yet where he was now wasn't really better. Glen wondered. Dad was a mechanic and that had been a great career, but these days TAFE mostly offered certificate courses for people who already had careers, like work health and safety or project management, or for disciplines mostly in the community sector like childcare, aged care or disability services, which were generally part-time, casual jobs not better than what Glen had now. One option though, although nobody in the family had ever worked in the field, was a business-based certificate from Young TAFE. That might be an opportunity and allow Glen to return home too.

"Glen," Charan said.

Glen looked up for Charan to hand across an envelope of cash, Glen's wages for his part-time, casual evening and night

34

shifts job at Parramatta North 7-11. There Charan waited as Glen opened his pay, counted out 200 dollars and handed that back. In the recent past, many small businesses like 7-11 franchise owners paid less than the award. Wages theft. When that became an issue, franchise owners were expected to pay the full award and sometimes were audited, so now they paid the full award but took part of each employee's wages back. Wages theft that couldn't be audited. Glen didn't want to give back 200 dollars but what could he do? Almost every job was casual or a gig contractor, where this job although casual had regular and good hours. If Glen didn't hand back his share, many more his age were waiting to take his place. Glen ought to be making enough but after he handed Charan's share back he wasn't making much at all.

Charan left. Glen worked the rest of his shift, mostly petrol sales, until Daniel arrived just before midnight to take over. After a quick hello and goodbye, Glen went to his car for his drive home on now quiet roads; around midnight was the only time roads in Sydney flowed well. Glen reached home to park his car in the unit complex carport, go to his unit and let himself inside. In no time Glen was in his bed and asleep.

* * *

Glen woke; checked his phone which was 9 04. Time to get up with his flatmate Andrew already at his work, daytimes at

Parramatta Woolworths. Glen showered, shaved and made breakfast before heading out to clear his head and buy milk.

Western Sydney was truly terrible. If there was a God and he made the ugliest city in the world, he put it in New South Wales and called it Sydney. Everyone knew Sydney's beaches, the opera house and the harbour bridge, but most of Sydney was a plain stretching ever westwards, with featureless house after featureless house after featureless house, and blocks of featureless units doing little to break an endless suburban monotony. Footpaths were lined by low brick front fences, behind which were front yards of grass. No trees, no shrubs, no flowers; just grass. Here and there were recreation reserves which were bigger plots of grass. Again no trees, no shrubs, no flowers; just grass. Shopping centres were always on the busier of roads of Sydney where traffic never stopped, except near midnight. But during the day, ugly shopping centres were an endless cacophony of traffic noise. Glen bought a two litre plastic bottle of milk before walking home. Sydney was awful, Glen didn't belong there, and although there were few job opportunities in his home town of Young, there were few decent job opportunities in Sydney. Glen reached home to put the milk in the fridge. There he pulled out his smartphone to browse the Young TAFE website. Glen scrolled their selection of full-year courses to find a Certificate Four in Accounting and Bookkeeping, and a Certificate Four in Business Administration which was probably more flexible. In Young he should be able to find a part-time job to pay his way while studying for a year, or actually two semesters so eight months, but if he didn't find a job he would be entitled Youth Allowance which would be enough to get by. That settled it.

Glen went to his contacts to text Josh. 'thinking coming home to do cert 4 in business administration at young tafe'.

Moments later: 'dont u like sydney'

'sydney no better than young so i will get skills to move to wagga for a good job'

'good idea'

'how are u'

'met a nice girl'

Typical of Josh. He had Emma as his girlfriend, the nicest and the prettiest of their year at school, but he didn't feel right about her so they parted. Now a couple of weeks later Josh had a new girlfriend.

'shes from wagga her family set up business here'

'whats her name'

'sophie shes lovely has lovely family too'

'mum and kev'

'couldnt stand them anymore so moved out'

'understand see u soon'

'see u brother'

Glen felt relieved. With a certificate four he had a chance to get a decent job, especially if he moved to Wagga, while

Wagga was nice enough and still close to home. Close to Josh, Hannah and his friends. That decided it. Glen scrolled his contacts to ring and tell Mum of his plans. She wouldn't be ecstatic about Glen coming home, while living with Mum and Kev might be a problem. If that was a problem he could move out like Josh did. With a job or Youth Allowance he could do that. Glen braced himself to ring Mum and tell her his news.

## Chapter Four

Luke opened his locker to stow his backpack before changing into his uniform: a light blue shirt, dark blue trousers, a cap with a chequered band; then his velcro-fastened vest which had handcuffs, a radio, a first-aid kit, notebook and ballpoint, a taser and capsicum spray. Next, an extendable baton hooked to his belt. Finally a Glock 22 automatic pistol, where Luke checked the 15 round magazine before sliding it home and putting the pistol in the holster on his right thigh. Now Senior Constable Scott, Luke went to the Operations Room to greet Senior Sergeant Leon Fowler, Leon, and his partner, Constable Alice Hewson, Alice; newly off probation and choosing to stay in Young. For Luke originally from nearby Cowra, Young was home.

"Did anything happen overnight that we need to look into?" Luke asked.

"From the logs, last night was quiet," Leon said.

"Good. We'll do a few loops of the town and then patrol Boorowa and Lovell Streets on foot."

"See you both."

They headed out to their white Holden Commodore numbered 313 on the roof, where Luke and Alice were now Young 313. Luke slid behind the wheel, got comfortable as best he could given the gear he wore, belted up, started the engine and headed out.

"What do you think for today?" Luke asked.

"Unroadworthy cars with burned-out tail lights."

"Shoplifting for an insurance report," Alice said.

"A break and enter, for insurance too."

"Drinking by Burrangong Creek."

With not enough jobs and nothing much to do all day, public drunkenness was sometimes a problem, as was petty stealing to pay for drugs. Luke thought more. "Car theft."

"A lot of older cars here, easy to steal. Hooning on public roads."

"Yeah. That just about covers it."

"Life on patrol in Young."

"Someone has to do it."

"There are worse places. How's your renovation going?" Alice asked.

"Slowly," Luke said.

Alice laughed. "Always slowly!"

"It's a lovely, old house."

"It sure is, and affordable."

"It's five minutes from work and no more than ten minutes from everywhere else."

"That too."

Cruising, cruising; Luke concentrating on driving and Alice concentrating on possible, petty crimes."

"Young 313," VKG, actually Sally, called over the radio.

Alice picked up the microphone. "Young 313."

"Code India; reported disturbance at Headspace in Boorowa Street."

"Five minutes," as Alice flicked lights and siren switches.

"Acknowledged."

Luke accelerated to a fast cruising speed as other motorists pulled over to give him a free run, although Young traffic was rarely busy. At the roundabout Luke went straight on to Headspace, where he double-parked while Alice switched off their siren but left their lights flashing, as was protocol. Out of the car to run inside, which was turmoil as Chloe, the only counsellor, cowered in the corner while Jake Turner, a known methamphetamine user, picked up the water cooler to smash it. Luke pulled out his taser; the best weapon for this.

"Jake, calm down!" Luke ordered.

"Fuck you!" was the response.

"What brought this on?" Luke asked Chloe.

"He needed a hit but I wouldn't give him money."

"Yeah, alright," Luke said. Chloe was pro-decriminalisation but the illegal drug problem had two sides, such as this chaos.

"Jake!" Alice ordered with her taser ready. "Just calm down."

"Fuck you too!"

"Swearing at us isn't getting you anywhere," Luke said.

"Yeah, well...."

"Lay down on the floor, hands behind your head."

"Fuck off."

"Jake!" Luke warned as he stepped closer with his taser now holstered and his baton extended.

"Come here Jake and I'll give you some money," Alice said. "How much? Fifty?"

The price for a point. Jake Turner lost focus to now advance on Alice.

"Stop there now!" Alice ordered.

But Jake Turner didn't stop so Luke hit him with his baton. Once, twice; for Jake to crumple. On the floor surrounded by broken crockery, Luke put his knee on Jake's back to snap handcuffs in place. There he pulled Jake, now docile, to his feet.

"Thanks Luke and Alice," Chloe said. "Ice is usually harmless....."

"So you say," Luke interrupted.

"When they're spaced out they're fine."

"What brought this on?"

"When addicts are coming down, anything can set them off."

"Yeah, right. A few hours in the cells, a charge of destruction of private property and a probable suspended sentence will see Jake Turner back here soon enough."

"He has a habit now out of control and not enough money to pay for it," Chloe said. She paused. "Thanks for helping me."

"Just doing our job," Alice said. "See you Chloe."

"See you Alice."

Alice opened their patrol car back door for Luke to shove Jake Turner into the back seat, while locals stopped and stared. Behind the wheel Luke buckled up. The damage to Headspace was minor and Chloe was unharmed. The worst part of this incident would be the time taken to prepare their report, and preparing paperwork to charge Jake Turner, including formally interviewing Chloe. Luke started the car while Alice switched off still flashing lights.

"We didn't say drug addict smashing-up youth counselling service," Alice said.

That was true. "We didn't," Luke agreed.

"No real harm done."

That was fortunate. Luke checked for traffic before pulling into Boorowa Street to drive to Young Police Station.

## Chapter Five

Thursday was the second of Josh's three working days, and that Thursday was quite hot. Josh drove to Blackett Avenue where he part-opened the window of his car a few centimetres before locking it with the remote. Like yesterday he used the knocker, to be greeted by Sophie even more barely dressed: this time in a red bikini top and tight, tiny denim shorts once more. That was it, no shoes even.

"Hi Josh," Sophie greeted.

"Hi Sophie."

"I'll beat you again!" she exclaimed.

Josh chuckled at that as he followed to her room where she shut the door behind. This time their controllers were waiting on the bed but Josh wasn't interested in that. Sophie's breasts, nicely sized and now mostly exposed, her tight shorts, her long legs. Josh stood toe to toe, as close as he should.

"Can I kiss you?" Josh asked.

"You can kiss me."

Josh hugged Sophie's waist, kissed her, cupped her bottom and kissed her again, felt himself growing, straining, aching.

"Can I touch your breasts?" Josh asked.

"Yes you can."

Josh moved one hand to her bikini top which had a bow. Josh pulled the knot for the top to release while Sophie hugged him tighter. With her top loosened Josh put his hands on her smooth, firm breasts which felt so good, and her hard nipples too. He cupped and massaged her there, totally gorgeous, but there was more.

"Can I touch between your legs?" Josh asked.

"Yes you can."

Still kissing, Josh moved his fingers to the button on her shorts, but they too tight! He tried but had no hope. Sophie eased away to unbutton them, also with some difficulty, and unzip them too. They fell to her ankles revealing red panties coloured like her bikini top. Now Josh hugged with his hands inside her panties cupping soft, round buttocks.

"Do you want to lie together naked?" Josh asked.

"Yes."

Josh stepped back, took Sophie's hand and led her to her bed to sit and then to lie. Josh pulled Sophie's panties down to be surprised. She wasn't shaved but instead was trimmed blonde.

One last question. "Do you want have sex with me?" Josh asked.

"Yes – everything," Sophie gasped.

Josh loosened his shirt before loosening and unzipping his long trousers, to lie gently against Sophie to kiss her while she hugged the bare skin of his back under his shirt. He kissed the side of Sophie's neck while she slid her hands under the waist of his trousers and underwear to hold his bottom. Sophie Weaver was the most beautiful girl in the world.

\* \* \*

Josh curled against Sophie's smooth, soft body. Slowly he became aware he was thirsty. Then Josh became aware that sort-of, just happened after Sophie agreed. It was nice, particularly it felt nice, but he hoped it was alright. But if there were problems for Sophie there were ways to fix that.

"Are you thirsty?" Sophie murmured.

"Yes I am."

"I have lemon, lime and bitters."

"I'll have whatever's easiest for you."

Sophie eased away, not easy when squashed into a single bed, and climbed down. There she pulled on her panties before opening the door and heading out.

"SOPHIE!" Jessica shouted while Josh wasn't surprised. Josh sat up where, on the cabinet next to her bed, was a smartphone, a purse, a bong, and a cigarette lighter. What a surprise! Sophie returned carrying two glasses wet with condensation. She gave one to Josh before putting the other on the cabinet next to the bong. She climbed beside Josh before grabbing her glass. Josh sipped; it was nice. No, not just nice.

"This is great," he said, but that wasn't enough. Sex, sweet drinks: everything. "You're great Sophie, I really like you."

"You're great Josh." Sophie looked into Josh's eyes. "I like you a lot."

"Do you want to be my girlfriend?" Josh asked.

"Yes I do."

Josh put his arm around Sophie while wondering how to raise the subject of the bong. That would make a memorable afternoon even more memorable.

"Do you want to do more?" Josh asked.

"Can you?"

"No, not that, the um...," Josh said as he looked towards her cabinet.

"Oh! Yeah, I'll get some. I have to run the gauntlet of Mum though."

"You could get dressed."

Sophie laughed. "That wouldn't be as much fun!"

Sophie slipped out of bed again, and still just wearing her panties she left the room. This time Jessica didn't shout at her. Sophie returned with another bong, a lighter and two ziplock bags.

"Do you...?" Josh asked.

"Just sometimes. And you?"

"Just once every couple of weeks."

"About the same for me. Base?"

Methamphetamine; Josh started with weed once in a while before he was given a bag of free base, or ice as he knew it. "Base is fine."

Sophie's bongs were nicely made in glass with coloured stripes. Josh watched as Sophie carefully poured the rocks of ice down the mouthpiece of the bong she held before she gave it and a lighter to Josh. He waited while she did the same to the bong from the cabinet beside her bed, and grabbed that lighter too. When Sophie lit her flame Josh did the same, before bringing the bong to his lips while allowing the flame to play over the bowl while circling the flame and rolling the bong to inhale the smoke of the melting ice. Nothing for a moment until it steadily washed over Josh, his tiredness after sex just disappeared and his calmness after sex became ever calmer. Significantly calm, settled, aware. Aware of everything, especially the scent of sex in the small room, the scent of Sophie alongside him. Simply: peacefulness, serenity and tranquillity beyond reason, logic or understanding. Josh inhaled the smoke to heal him; heal him to his core. He loved this feeling which was why he rationed it, to make it special. Perpetual peacefulness would lose its appeal just as sex every day would lose its attraction. But a few hours of bliss once a fortnight was amazing.

Josh held his empty bong with his fingertips, feeling almost bursting horny. Naked but for her panties pressed skin to skin on her bed, Josh really wanted her. No, he ached for her.

"Do you want to have sex again?" Josh asked.

"Fuck yeah!"

Sophie slid down the bed before pulling her panties off. Josh slid down to lie side by side and lifted her leg, slid his leg under and guided himself inside. So nice intertwined like that. Josh could have lasted all night and he probably would.

That was nice and normally Sophie would have liked it, but not that time. She wanted more, no, she needed more.

"Fuck me hard, Josh," Sophie murmured, but he didn't. "Fuck me hard," Sophie said, but still no change. "Fuck me hard, Josh!" she ordered.

Josh slid out, momentarily Sophie felt empty; he climbed on top and slid in, and then she was deliciously full. Josh fucked her steady then harder, then harder still, then really hard, then really, really hard. Sweaty hard, his sweat dripping on her face, on her body; manly sweat fucking her hard. Sophie felt it slowly building: bigger and bigger, brighter and brighter, more and more until it burst free. Big, big, massively big. As she slowly came back from her orgasm, Josh was still fucking her hard, pounding her into her bed. Sophie felt it buzzing faintly; she turned her head and closed her eyes. Building and building more and more, brighter and brighter and then it overflowed. Big, big pleasure. And still Josh fucked her, his sweat dripping, her bed creaking.

"Come for me Josh," Sophie murmured while she grabbed his buttocks tight like a spring. Every muscle in his body wound tight, so tight. "Come, come now, come Josh." Hard, harder, bed creaking, Josh grunting on each stroke. Louder and louder, harder and harder until the biggest. More and more and more until he collapsed on her. Sweaty body pressed against sweaty body. *Fuck that was good!*

Sophie held Josh as she slowly became aware of more than just fucking. Blissful or peaceful or satisfied didn't begin to describe how she felt. Love. She loved Josh, she loved sex, she loved the world, she loved everybody and everything. Overflowing with love for life. As Josh moved Sophie became even more aware. She reached for her phone – fuck! Then she remembered.

"We better get ready for dinner," Sophie said.

"What time is it?"

"Seven-eleven."

"That late!"

"Wait here for a moment and I'll talk with Mum and Jack."

"Are you sure this is alright. I mean...."

Of course Mum and Jack knew what was going on, but Sophie was old enough and Josh was now her boyfriend. Which meant another thing which Sophie had to sort out.

Sophie pulled on her panties and shorts before slipping on her top.

"Can you tie this please?"

Josh did, before Sophie dashed from her room straight into the stern frown of Mum.

"What have you been doing?" Mum hissed.

"Josh is now my boyfriend," Sophie said.

"But you're only 16!"

"How old were you when you had me?"

In the background Jack lurked but kept away from mother and daughter.

"I'm old enough to have a boyfriend, I'm old enough to do that, and I've taken precautions," Sophie said to no response. "This is what boyfriends and girlfriends do, as I'm sure you remember." Still no response. "I much rather here than in the back of his car or somewhere like that. Just because you're not aware doesn't mean it won't be happening."

Mum's face softened. "I suppose so. If you're taking precautions, alright."

"I love him, you know."

Mum sort-of smiled. "You could do worse."

"Jack," Sophie said. "I know we followed Josh around, and I bought the rake to invite him here so we could find out if can help your business. I now know Josh can help you, but I don't want Josh to think I invited him just because of that. Well, I did invite him because of that but now I've fallen in love, if that makes sense. In any case we'll get him to help you but don't ask tonight."

"Okay Sophie. Can he help us?"

"He uses every few weeks and he's lived here all his life, as we know."

"When the time's right we'll ask."

"One thing Sophie," Mum said firmly. "Your room is your room and I won't interfere, but don't walk around this house just wearing your panties ever again!"

That *was* the wrong thing to do; perhaps Sophie was high on love or something. "I understand. Are we too late for dinner?"

"Jack's doing a barbeque. Josh can help him."

"And we'll do the salads."

Mum shook her head while smiling.

"I'll get Josh," Sophie said. She returned to Josh now fully dressed. "All good," she said.

"Really?" Josh exclaimed. "No, that's great. Your mother's great."

"You're my boyfriend so this is how it will be. Now, you're going to help Jack cook a barbeque while we make some salads."

"Sophie Weaver, I really love you and your family."

"I love you too, Josh...," and she frowned.

"Josh Ward."

"I love you Josh Ward. Now, you have a barbeque to cook and cars to talk about."

"Not that orange car!"

Sophie smiled brightly. Better Josh than her!

# Chapter Six

Fridays were the busiest days of the week at work. All the farmers came to town, identified by sundried skin and Akubra hats. Josh helped seven farmers, but it was unusual when late in his working day he sensed someone in the next aisle. Farmers had to drive home so they rarely shopped late. Josh went around the corner to a pleasant surprise: Sophie. Unexpectedly pleasant given they agreed to meet on Saturday.

"Hi Sophie. Looking for another rake?" Josh asked.

"Hi Josh," Sophie said. "The rake's fine, um, it's just I was lonely and I thought – well, here I am!"

That was nice. Sex was nice, sex with drugs was even nicer, but to be thought about when lonely was the nicest of all. Josh glanced at the clock with 20 minutes to go.

"Josh...?" John asked.

Josh turned to face his boss and owner of the store. "John, this is my girlfriend Sophie."

John shook hands with Sophie while nodding his head in appreciation. "Pleased to meet you, Sophie."

"Pleased to meet you, John."

"It's nearly time, Josh," John said. "You might as well go."

"Thanks John, see you."

"See you next week.'

They headed out to Boorowa Street.

"He seems nice," Sophie said.

"Yeah, John's nice." Josh bent his head close. "He admired you the day you bought that rake.'

"That's fine."

Josh guessed Sophie was used to being admired. They reached Josh's car where he took the remote from his pocket while thinking. "I need to go home to get a few things, so I'll introduce you to Mum and Kev if that's alright."

"That's a good idea."

Josh knew that wasn't a good idea but it was something he should do. He pressed the remote and they climbed into baking heat, as expected for a car sitting in the sun for several hours. With airconditioning making little difference in the ten minute drive home, Josh parked in the street. Hand in hand they went to the front door where Josh used his keys to go inside to smoky mustiness and semi-darkness.

"Hannah?" Mum's voice called.

"It's me, Mum," Josh replied.

"The prodigal son." Mum appeared in the corridor, cigarette hanging from her mouth. "Who's this?"

"Mum, this is my new girlfriend Sophie Weaver."

"Pleased to meet you," Sophie greeted with her hands clasped behind her back.

"Raiding the kindergarten, Josh?" Mum asked.

"Sophie's in high school, Mum. She's old enough."

"Old enough to be a half-naked slut."

"It's hot outside," Sophie said.

"Did you bring your schoolgirl home to fuck her?" Mum asked.

"I came home to get some things."

"So you're fucking your schoolgirl somewhere else?"

Josh didn't expect this; worse than Emma used to get. Far worse. Josh couldn't understand why Mum hated Sophie this way. He tried to get his thoughts in order.

"We're in love," Josh said, "that's all."

"Love or lust?"

"I'm no expert but this is love."

"Who's that?" Kev asked before he appeared in the corridor, smoking too.

"Kev, this is my new girlfriend Sophie Weaver."

"This is Josh's schoolgirl slut," Mum said.

"Come on Laura," Kev said. "Hello Sophie," Kev then greeted pleasantly.

"Hello Kev," Sophie said quietly.

"I came home to get some things and introduce Sophie to you both," Josh said.

"Thank you Josh," Kev said.

Josh eased Sophie past Mum and Kev to lead her to his room where he grabbed a calico bag for the rest of his shirts and jeans. Sophie watched from the doorway. Josh reached behind Sophie to close the door.

"I'm sorry about that," he said quietly.

"It's not your fault."

"If we never met my mum that would have seemed odd. So now you've met her."

"Why does she hate me? Am I dressed wrong?"

Sophie wore tiny denim shorts and a blue halter top. That might have been part of the problem, although Mum treated Emma badly too. "If this was winter and you were dressed in jeans and a pullover it still would have been bad."

"She's your mum."

"She's my mum which is why I keep my distance. I'm sleeping on a couch at a mate's place."

Sophie put her hand to her mouth. "Really?"

"If I'm living here, things might be said or done that aren't right."

"That's good of you, Josh."

"Maybe one day things will turn better," Josh said, although he didn't believe things would ever turn better. Josh then wondered what to do for the rest of their evening. He couldn't take Sophie to James' house; that was intrusive for a family that was more than generous to him. There was one option for a Friday night. "Do you play pool?" Josh asked.

"I've never tried."

"How about we go to The Australian? I'll teach you to play pool and later we'll have a counter meal. Do you drink?"

"Not beer."

"Me neither. A couple of ciders, no, a glass of wine with a steak?"

"For an underage drinker?"

"You're old enough, Sophie Weaver."

"Pool, a steak and a glass of wine sounds great."

Josh slung the calico bag over his shoulder before taking Sophie's hand to enter a now empty corridor. They reached the front door.

"See you Mum and Kev," Josh shouted to silence.

Still hand in hand they walked to Josh's old Commodore.

# Chapter Seven

Sophie woke early Saturday morning, didn't know what time, but all was dark and quiet outside. Out of nowhere she had the answer for dealing with Josh, from something he told them. First she needed to speak with Jack, and then she could do what Jack wanted while not alerting Josh that their initial meeting wasn't accidental. Even better that she could fix one of Josh's problems in life. Pleased, Sophie rolled onto her other side to sleep, except sleep wouldn't come.

Eventually she slept to wake when bright sunlight seeped around her blind. In her pyjamas Sophie went to shower and wash her hair, towel herself dry and use the dryer, before returning to her room. There Sophie opened her wardrobe before going to her Galaxy S10 to check Weatherzone. The forecast was 34 and sunny, so she pondered. Sophie had three pairs of denim shorts but Josh had seen those, and she had white shorts but wanted a different look. She flicked through her dresses and skirts before something caught her eye. A black, leather mini skirt would be good for a hot day. She checked her shoes where sandals with wedge-shaped cork heels caught her eye. Classy, sexy and practical. She laid those out before thinking about tops. Sophie didn't like t-shirts, everyone wore t-shirts so she didn't. Her skirt was tight so the top needed to be tight too. A white halter with no bra because straps would show. That was it, laid on her bed. Sophie then wondered why she dressed to impress.

Probably from Mum who was in good shape and who dressed to impress. Not shorts so much, more tight jeans, tight yoga pants, and sometimes miniskirts. That was Mum's style and that was Sophie's style too. Once dressed Sophie went to the kitchen where she had another decision to make. She flicked on the electric kettle, grabbed a frypan, spread some oil and put it on the stove before cracking an egg. While that was cooking she put two slices of bread in the toaster, before the kettle switched off so she made coffee with milk and sugar. The toaster almost threw her toast onto the bench just as her egg was ready, so with a plate, and a knife and fork, Sophie had breakfast.

"Well, you've been busy!" Mum exclaimed as she entered the kitchen.

"Breakfast," Sophie said.

"Looks good." Mum sat opposite. "You're growing up, Sophie. Cooking, now a boyfriend, and a good one too. One word of advice: if over time you aren't going well together, don't try to force it. If it's not right it's not going to last."

Sophie guessed what that was about. "Like you and Dad?"

"We started well and he was a nice guy but we didn't have enough in common."

Sophie shrugged her shoulders. Love was new to her so breakups were beyond what she could comprehend.

"Don't stress," Mum said. "What you have now might go the distance and good luck if it does. Just if at any time if it doesn't feel right then it probably isn't."

Sophie sort-of understood. "Thanks Mum." She finished her egg and toast. "Where's Jack."

"In the garage."

*Where else?* Sophie washed her plates and the frypan before putting them away, getting another commendation from Mum, then went to Jack pondering the engine of his Charger.

"Hi Jack, can we talk?" Sophie asked.

"Sure," he said as he emerged from mechanical components that didn't make sense to Sophie in the slightest.

"I think I have a way of getting what you need from Josh, if you tell me what you want."

"Yeah, sure. I need to know who the dealers in Young are, for interest's sake, and I want to give samples and our address to existing users to get us established."

"So you need to know who these users are?"

"Yeah."

"What are you going to sell?"

"Weed, base, coke and China girl. Weed and base are the easiest to get, the others I can do but with more difficulty."

"Anyone can cook methamphetamine."

"Most of our stuff comes from China."

"Ecky?" Sophie asked.

Jack frowned. "I can't imagine dance clubs in Young."

"House parties: a bit of music, a bit of drinking, a bit of drugs. Someone goes there with a bundle of packets."

"Until the police show up because a neighbour has phoned in a noisy party."

"If it's noise they're not interested in drugs."

"Are you sure?"

"I've seen weed and ecky and police weren't interested at all."

"I can do ecky."

"Good. I'll speak with Josh and tell him what you want."

"Are you sure?"

"Josh has to earn his fair share. One-quarter of any business he brings in."

Jack frowned. "Alright," he eventually said.

"If Josh were to move in here, would you have a problem?"

"He's a nice guy and if he can help us, then no. But you better check with your mother."

"I will, but it's just what we've got now but one step further."

"School?"

"Josh passed year 12 so he can help me."

"Talk with your mother."

"I will." Sophie laughed. "Look after that car, Jack."

"It's losing coolant from somewhere."

Sophie shook her head as she left the garage. In the kitchen Mum sat at the small table with a mug of coffee. Sophie switched on the kettle which was still hot, before making herself a mug. She sat with Mum and drank some.

"How are you Mum?"

"I'm fine Sophie. What do you want?"

Sophie wasn't surprised by that question. "I'm going to ask Josh to help our business and in turn he'll take a share what he brings in." Sophie sipped more coffee. "I met Josh's mother so I know why he's staying with a friend. Actually, he sleeps on a couch. I would like him to stay with us."

"No Sophie."

"Why not?"

"You're only 16 and you have school."

"But I feel grown-up and school won't be a problem. If Josh comes to visit and stay for dinner a couple of times a week, that's going to take more time than – you know."

"Just fucking?"

"No, it's not just fucking," Sophie said. "It's good – great." Sophie decided another way. "Josh passed year 12 not so long ago and he can help me with my assignments." Still no response. "I like him and I know he likes me."

"Yeah, you two are good together."

"It's just what we've agreed but one step more."

"It's a big step Sophie."

"If we work we work, and if we don't we don't, but it would be good for Josh, good for the business and good for me."

Mum shook her head. "I must be a bad mother."

Sophie put her hand on Mum's hand. "I've met lots of mothers and you're the best. Jack loves you, I love you; I love you more than I can describe."

"I mustn't be so bad after all. You say Josh is sleeping on a couch."

"That's better than living with his mother."

"Is she that bad?"

"She's really bad. She hates me even though I just met her."

Mum drank the last of her coffee. "That's bad for Josh and he's a good guy too. Okay, I agree on two conditions. You can only go out on weekends, not weekday nights, and you must get B or at least C on all of your assignments."

Sophie barely believed that. "And Josh can stay?"

"If you can make this work and if it doesn't affect your schoolwork, then Josh can live here. I'll buy you a present, a queen-sized bed."

"Thanks Mum."

"You'll be the only girl in year 12 living with her boyfriend."

"They used to get married at 16," Sophie said. "My grandparents did."

"If you add up the dates your grandma was pregnant too."

Sophie laughed. "Really?"

"Don't tell anyone. Do girls your age have boyfriends?" Mum asked.

"Not so much year 11, but in year 12 I saw couples. It's natural, after all."

"You might be right about this being less disruptive than dating, and Josh can help with your schoolwork too. I know he'll do that if you ask him."

Sophie felt light-headed and more ecstatic than she'd ever felt before. "This is just so good!" she exclaimed.

"This is called love, Sophie, and there isn't an age limit I suppose. It took me a while and a few mistakes, but if you feel it here," Mum said with her hand over her heart, "it's real."

At that moment Sophie felt it everywhere.

* * *

Josh lay on his back with Sophie curled into his side. His plan was to start their next mission in Call of Duty: Modern Warfare, but Sophie's tiny leather miniskirt which barely covered her bottom, and her tight white halter which showed everything right down to erect nipples, led to other things. Not that Josh minded: more than beautiful and sexy Sophie was great that way. She was great in every way.

"You're currently staying with a friend," Sophie said. "Is it good for you to get out of your friend's house for today?"

64

Josh couldn't perpetually hang around another family. "Yes, it is," he agreed.

"Well, we've got all day today. The base we smoked the other day; that came from Jack. That's what he sells."

Josh was staggered. "Really?" he exclaimed.

"That's the business Jack was talking about. Too much competition in Wagga but he was told there's less competition here."

"There are two dealers I know of," Josh said while he thought. "Daniel Stewart and Mike Kelly."

"Do you think there are others?"

"I'm fairly sure there aren't."

"To get started he needs to know some users."

"That's easy enough."

"For you?"

"Yes."

"Do you mind?"

"What?"

"Give them free samples and this address. You get one-quarter of any business you bring in."

Josh took a deep breath while he thought that through, but Daniel lived a normal, domestic life selling drugs. If users didn't buy from Daniel they would buy from someone else. No harm involved, just a different seller, while earning his share would be useful given he barely got by on the hours he worked. Josh thought that through again with the same clarity. "No problem," Josh eventually said.

"Now, instead of staying with your friend would you like to move in here?"

"Here, here?" Josh asked.

"Here in this bedroom here. We'll get a bigger bed."

Josh barely believed that while Sophie moved to sit cross-legged. "Mum and Jack say we can. If we work we work, and if we don't we don't, but apart from the cost of a bigger bed...."

Josh realised he was smiling brightly. "I would like to move in here with you," he said. Then he thought. "What's Jack selling?"

"Weed, base, coke, China girl and ecky. The base is good as you know, from China."

"Do you want to start today?"

"You're joking?"

"Let's make a day of it. You were dressed up, I was dressed up, so we'll go to the Chinese Gardens, hand out some samples and this address, and later eat out. My treat."

"Sure, seeing as you're now one-quarter of a drug dealer!"

That was true.

"What do you think about selling drugs?" Josh asked out of curiosity.

"If people want drugs they'll get them one way or the other. We were selling in Wagga."

She didn't show it but Sophie was brought up in the world of drug-dealing, like Daniel's children Tracy and Mia. In time, Tracy and Mia would think selling drugs was as normal as selling a garden rake. Now it was time to get going. "Let's dress, see Jack, and then head off to the Chinese Gardens."

Sophie frowned. "Why do they have Chinese Gardens in Young?"

"Back in the really old days, Young was called Lambing Flat and they mined alluvial gold here. Chinese did that well while Europeans struggled to extract enough gold to make their efforts worthwhile. You can guess where this went: persecution followed by a number of anti-Chinese riots. The government moved in to restore order and the Chinese here were able to stay on, but after that Chinese and Asian immigration was banned to New South Wales, and then to Australia for more than 100 years. The Chinese Gardens are a tribute to the Chinese who stayed on in what's now called Young. There are some good Chinese restaurants here if you're interested."

"I'm interested in a good Chinese restaurant perhaps this evening. You know everything about Young. I have one question about Young: most towns are built on a river."

"Burrangong Creek fills that role." He saw Sophie's eyes roll, no doubt thinking about the broad Murrumbidgee River flowing through Wagga. "Like many things in Young,

Burrangong Creek tries but it doesn't quite get there."
Enough of that. "We need to get going, Sophie."

She slid out of bed to pull on her panties, halter top, miniskirt and sandals, and then a black corduroy peaked cap which was too cool. Josh dressed in a t-shirt, long lightweight slacks and runners; practical for a hot day. He thought more about their day.

"Could you make a picnic lunch?" Josh asked.

"Egg sandwiches?" Sophie offered.

"Perfect!"

"Josh Ward, we're good together."

"We are."

* * *

The wealthy in Young lived on two, three, four and even five hectare blocks on the outskirts of the town, in massive houses with massive garages and sheds, surrounded by immaculate gardens and lawns tended by professional gardeners. To the east of the town centre In the midst of that was the Lambing Flat Chinese Tribute Garden at Chinaman's Dam, which was a sizeable lake. Gently undulating countryside, lawn as immaculate as any of the wealthy houses nearby, ducks, swans, and across a bridge on an island, the Chinese Gardens. For some reason Josh's friends from school went there most Saturday's especially when the weather was nice, which that day certainly was. Josh parked amongst 20 or 30 cars.

"This is lovely!" Sophie exclaimed as she climbed out to view the gardens in the near distance: guarded by two stone lions either side of a Chinese gate in red.

It was lovely as Josh looked all around before he spotted them. He took Sophie's hand to lead her to six boys and five girls all Josh's age: 19. The girls, like many Australian girls, were mostly a bit plump to fat while some of the boys weren't much better. Josh strode up to the group on the shore of the lake under the shade of a gum tree, aware of the packets he carried. He knelt so Sophie knelt too.

"I'll do introductions," Josh said. "James knows I've been busy these past few days, because of Sophie here. Sophie, these are James, Matt, Emma, Alana, Leah, Justin, Toby, Noah, Lucas, Charlotte and Zoe. My friends, this is Sophie Weaver new in Young from Wagga Wagga, my girlfriend."

Greetings were exchanged while Emma stayed silent, as to be expected.

Sophie didn't sit on the grass; her dress was clearly too short and tight for that, so she continued to kneel while Josh sat to relax. He gave one bag of base to James.

"What's this for?" James asked.

"That's a sample for you. When you want more, see Jack or me at 37 Blackett Avenue."

"Ah."

"Top quality and good prices."

"Pure?"

"The best from China."

James laughed. "That's appropriate!"

Then a packet of base to Matt. "You know the address."

"For next time, yeah. Credit?"

"Sorry, no credit."

Next packet of base was for Emma.

"Discount for a friend?" she asked.

"It's 40 dollars, and if you ring me we'll deliver."

She nodded her head.

"Will we be seeing you?" Josh asked Emma.

"Better to buy from a friend," Emma said

That was 'yes'. Next packet, China girl for Alana.

"Thanks Josh. Don't worry, I'll be seeing you."

"Thanks."

Next packet, base for Leah.

"Thanks Josh."

Finally two packets of coke for Lucas and Zoe, holding hands as always. Josh then sat with the remaining packets in his lap.

"What about me?" Justin asked in a hurt voice.

"What do you want Justin: base, coke, ecky or China girl? We also do weed but I don't have samples."

"There's a party at our place tonight."

"Really?"

"You're welcome, and your girlfriend."

"Thanks. Josh took a packet from the bundle. "You'll need this," as he handed over a packet with two ecky tablets. "Remember, 37 Blackett Avenue."

"Singed in here," Justin said as he tapped his forehead.

"Toby?" who wasn't a school friend.

"No, I'm good."

"You'll be at the party?"

"Sure."

"Charlotte?"

"I've been known to more than just party."

Josh smiled as he handed her ecky. "Remember, there's more where that came from."

"I'll remember."

"Anyone else?" Josh asked. "Older brothers and sisters, younger brothers and sisters?"

"Parents?" Zoe asked while Josh couldn't help but stare at her. "Mum and Dad do lines before fucking on Saturday nights." She looked at Josh. "I came home unexpectedly and they were in the living room."

"Would it be embarrassing for you to tell them about better quality and cheaper prices?"

"Not as embarrassing as that Saturday night! No, I'll let Dad know."

Josh casually tossed a bag of coke to Zoe.

"My boyfriend," Alana said.

"Same as you?"

"Yeah."

Josh gave Alana another packet of China girl.

"Who's this boyfriend?" James asked.

"Mike's older," she said. "Thirties."

"Too old for us here on Saturdays," James said.

"Yes he is, but he's right for me."

"My brother Mark and his girlfriend," Lucas said."

"Coke like you?"

"Yeah."

Josh tossed two packets across. "Don't forget, 37 Blackett Avenue."

"I'll see them on the way home and let them know."

"Thanks."

"Anyone else?"

Silence so that covered it.

"Now who's connected to who?" Sophie asked.

"Toby and I," Justin said proudly while Sophie nodded her head.

"Charlotte and I," Noah said.

"Zoe and I," Lucas said.

"My boyfriend Mike who's not here," Alana said, clearly wanting those who missed it the first time to know about Mike.

"That's it," Josh said while catching the eye of Emma.

"What are you doing here in Young?" Emma asked Sophie.

"I'll be doing year 12 next year."

"Still in school?"

"Yes, but there are things they don't teach you in school."

James laughed, as did Justin and Toby.

The group discussion was Matt was thrown out by his mother to end up couch-surfing with Leah, who was just as addicted as he was, and how tough they were doing it on Newstart and probably stealing from Leah's family until they eventually ran out of patience and threw her out too. Maybe that made Matt and Leah a couple but Josh doubted they could do much in their drug-induced hazes. The rest worked casual part-time in retail, travel agents or cafes. One of those cafes, the Art of Espresso, was where Justin met, and Josh guessed fell in love, with Toby. Young, New South Wales, had reached the year 2019.

"Do you want to look at the gardens?" Josh asked Sophie.

"Sure."

Josh stood, as did Sophie.

"Don't forget...," Josh said.

"37 Blackett Avenue," James Interrupted and laughed with most of the others joining in.

Josh headed across the lush, green grass with Sophie by his side.

"Who was your girl?" she asked.

"Why do you say that?" Josh asked.

"That wasn't your first time with me."

"I dated Emma for a while."

"I sensed something from her."

That was complicated. "Emma was serious but I didn't feel quite right about us together. Then it didn't feel right to keep dating when she wanted more."

"I understand. Mum and Dad weren't suited and we had a talk about that. Don't try to make something out of what's not there."

Josh nodded his head while he thought Jessica was right. His Mum and Dad were the same, and although Mum and Kev weren't suited either, but at least Dad hadn't been happier than these past few years. They crossed the bridge, between the lions and under the gate.

"This is really nice here," Sophie said. "Later we'll have sandwiches."

They walked through the gardens, like being in Beijing even.

"You met Mum and Kev yesterday which I'm sure you'll never forget! When we've got time I'll introduce you to Dad and Jenny," Josh said. "They're nice. Jenny's not much older than you."

"Age isn't a barrier when it comes to attraction."

"We're only a few years different."

"That wasn't what Emma was thinking!"

Personality mattered more than looks although Emma was the best of them as regards looks; in particular she had magnificent tits. They walked through the gardens around the circumference of the small island, stopped to admire the reproduction ancient brass horse from near Beijing, before crossing the bridge to Josh's car, where a plastic container of sandwiches and a glass bottle of ginger cordial mixed with water were retrieved.

"What is it with you and cordial?" Josh asked.

"It's nice."

They sat at a table.

"What's next?" Sophie asked.

"A few house calls. Later we'll go to the Mandarin Court for dinner."

"And then a party."

"Yeah."

"I'll get stuff from Jack before we go there." Sophie ate more of her sandwich. "If half the people this morning come good, you're going to make good money. Add to that the party tonight."

"That's mine?" Josh asked.

"Your friend invited you to his party, not Jack or me."

That was true.

"One thing you'll have to get used to beyond cordial is I like eggs," Sophie said.

"This sandwich is lovely." Josh thought about selling ecky tonight, which was something he never would have thought about. "You had it right when you said there are things not learned in school."

Sophie smiled brightly.

"I think I love you, Sophie Weaver."

"I think I love you too, Josh Ward."

* * *

At nine at night, late dusk and under the streetlights of Cowper Street, Sophie looked simply amazing. At home they got supplies for the party before changing, Josh to dress up in long trousers and a long-sleeved shirt, and Sophie having to change because she couldn't dance in a tight miniskirt. She chose a minidress with a plunging neckline so no bra, tight at her waist, and then frilly just covering her bottom. In stilettos the way her hips swayed caused her dress to show glimpses of her bottom on each stride, although she wore a g-string. Amazing look. Most girls looked awkward walking in shoes like that but Sophie's strides were just right.

"How did you learn to walk in those shoes?" Josh asked.

"Mum taught me."

No surprises there. Sophie's style was Jessica Weaver rewritten. They closed on number three with the sound of music audible but not loud enough to annoy neighbours. It was a large brick veneer on a hilly block with a single garage under; must have been a share house. The door was unlocked as Jack took Sophie's hand to ease into the crowd, for crowd it was. Crowded and pungent with weed although most there either had cans of beer or cans of mixer drinks. It was odd that one drug, alcohol, was freely available and even taxed while other drugs, often less harmful, were the scourge of the earth. Most stood in small groups talking while a few danced and Josh looked for his friends, but only saw Justin and Toby who were the centre of attention. Josh eased closer.

"Ah Josh," Justin said with a bright smile. "Your stuff is great!"

"Thanks. What's this party for?"

"Sorry; I didn't tell you. This is our engagement."

"Congratulations!" Josh exclaimed.

Sophie hugged Justin and hugged Toby too. "I'm so pleased."

"Love is love," Toby said.

"I've just learned about love."

"You too?"

"The real thing, everything!"

"I can see that."

You could see it in her smile.

"Congratulations," Josh repeated.

"Thanks Josh."

Josh eased Sophie away to give others access to the guests of honour. Who would have thought that in Young there would be a party for two men getting engaged? Not just a party but the biggest party for a long time.

"Where are the drinks?" Sophie asked Josh.

"Probably in the kitchen."

"Stupid me."

Easing through the crush to the bathroom actually, with a bath full of ice and beer cans. Josh watched Sophie who'd done this before, as she went to a girl close to the bath,

"That or ecky?" Sophie asked.

"How much?"

"Forty for two."

"Alright."

Cash was swapped for a packet retrieved from Sophie's black leather shoulder bag before she moved to a guy, while Josh decided to find the mixer drinks, which were in the kitchen in a couple of plastic rubbish bins filled with ice, surrounded by a fair-sized crowd.

"That or ecky?" Josh asked a girl.

"The real deal?"

"The best. Two for forty."

He worked his way through party goers retrieving drinks before returning to the crowded living room. There he saw Sophie working the room so he did the same from the other end. By then he was running low and also noticed Emma alone. He went to her.

"Hi Emma."

"Hi Josh. I'm pleased to see you're happy."

"Thanks."

Sophie came to them.

"Hi Sophie."

"Hi Emma.  Do you want to dance?"

"Seriously?"

"You should know men never dance.  Come on!"

Sophie virtually dragged Emma to the impromptu dance floor where the two girls, one amazingly beautiful and one totally attractive, really got into the music together.  Soon they had a crowd standing in a circle watching, including Justin and Toby enjoying the show which went on for a long time.  Eventually Emma pulled away looking half exhausted with a big smile.  Sophie came to Josh while Emma watched them still smiling.  Sophie had just made best friends with Josh's ex-girlfriend.

"She's nice," Sophie shouted in Josh's ear above ever-louder music.

"She was always nice," Josh shouted back.  "Not magical like you but nice."  Josh thought.  "Let's dance."

"Fuck yeah!"

They went to the dance floor and simply danced, and even though he didn't usually dance, Josh was glad he did.  As they danced amongst a few others dancing, including girls dancing with girls taking Sophie's and Emma's lead, it took someone quite out of the ordinary to break Josh's comfort zone and realise that dancing was fun when you just went with it.

Without doubt that was the best party that Josh had ever been to, as they danced the night away.

## Chapter Eight

Josh headed into the kitchen at close to midday for what was really lunch. The party ended quite late, it seemed because of the drugs they sold. As they took effect you could sense the atmosphere of warmth, love and affection. More and more and more.

The kitchen was original: white painted timber cupboards with cream laminate benchtops, an older-style electric stove, and a small stained pine timber table with two matching chairs. In the backyard Josh heard a lawnmower bellowing as Jack laboured on a spacious block. Josh sat at the table.

"Scrambled eggs, toast and coffee?" Sophie asked.

She was right about eggs. "That'll be fine."

Sophie set to cooking while Josh noticed her bag from last night on the table. The lawnmower stopped not long before Jack came inside, somewhat sweaty. He sat in the other chair.

"How did it go yesterday?" Jack asked.

"How many do you think?" Josh asked Sophie.

"In total including brothers, sisters, girlfriends, boyfriends and parents: 38."

"Fuck, sorry," Jack said. "The party?"

Sophie put Josh's plate and mug down, before going to her bag. She pulled out a wad of mostly 20 dollar bills and one packet.

"You sold all but one?" Jack asked incredulously.

"It was a big party," Sophie said.

Jack frowned while he flicked through the notes. "Fuck, 1,560!" He then flicked through them again before handing a smaller wad to Josh. "Your share."

"Thanks Jack." Josh put those notes in his trouser pocket.

Sophie went to the dining room to bring a chair from there. She sat between. "Any more ideas?"

Josh thought. "We missed three who were out yesterday so we'll try again this morning, no it's now afternoon. Those three might have more brothers, sisters and even parents. Then we'll visit Dad, Jenny and my sister."

"How old is she?" Sophie asked.

"Jade is three."

"Can you think of anything else?"

"Headspace is in Boorowa Street where clients come and go, and sometimes hang out at the park on Burrangong Creek near there. We could pay those clients a visit. Centrelink is in Lovell Street so we'll pay their clients a visit too. Tomorrow."

"These will be hardcore users."

"They will be."

"Jack, do you and Mum...?"

"What?"

"You know? Sample.'

"Casually."

"Fuck afterwards?"

"Sophie!"

She shrugged her shoulders.

"It's been known to happen," he said.

"Nice."

Josh finished his lunch for which Sophie took the plates to wash up.

"Josh, your family...?" Sophie asked while Josh admired her short, white shorts from behind.

"Mum and Kev drink too much, while Dad just has a beer every now and then." Josh thought. "We need a cover story for Dad for what we do here." He remembered the mowing. "Jack's running a gardening business."

"Good story," Sophie said. "I'm done here so let's go."

They headed into bright sunshine for what was sure to be a busy yet pleasant afternoon.

# Chapter Nine

Glen parked his Mitsubishi Mirage in the familiar driveway of a familiar house. He pressed the remote to lock his car before pressing the buzzer beside the front door. Inside, footsteps approached. Door opened with Mum smoking a cigarette.

"Hi Mum."

"Hi Glen, come in."

He entered the house dark after intense sunlight, and smelling musty and smoky.

"How are you?" Mum asked.

"I'm good."

"Hi Glen," Hannah greeted; standing behind Mum.

"Hi Hannah; how are you?"

"I'm enjoying my holidays! You know Josh is living with his girlfriend and she's my age."

"I know Josh has a girlfriend," Glen said, but he didn't know Sophie was 16 or 17.

"We might even be in the same classes next year," Hannah said.

"You might. Is she nice?"

"She's really nice."

Josh said Sophie was lovely and it seems he wasn't exaggerating.

"I hope you don't intend to sponge here," Mum said before drawing on her cigarette.

"I want to do a business certificate at the TAFE, and I'll get a part-time job or get Youth Allowance so I can pay board."

Mum drew on her cigarette again. "That'll be alright. You can have your old room."

"Thanks Mum. I'll get my things from the car."

"Things didn't work out in Sydney?"

"They did and I was fine, but I wasn't better off than living here, and here's better than Sydney. Less noisy and less crowded here; Sydney's awful that way."

Mum went into the living room to butt her cigarette on a brown ceramic ashtray on the low, coffee table. She turned to face Glen still in the corridor. "I hope you do better than your brother and his slut."

Glen wasn't surprised Mum said that. Life had treated her hard and she resented other people being happy. There wasn't anything Glen could say in response to that.

"I'll get my things from the car."

Glen headed out for his backpack and bag before returning for his big box which could only fit on the backseat. After unpacking in his old room which hadn't changed, Glen wondered what to do next. Get out of that house so he decided to visit Josh, but not tell Mum of course. He pulled out his iPhone and texted: 'arrived home can I visit'.

Moments later: 'come now and stay for dinner 37 Blackett St'.

'kk'.

"Going out Mum," Glen called as he headed to his car. There he pulled out his map, found Blackett Street, and set off for an older-style, fibro house in white. He used the knocker on the door, moments later to be greeted by Josh in jeans and a t-shirt.

"It's good you're home," Josh said with a bright smile

"It's good to be home."

"Come in and I'll introduce you to Sophie."

Glen followed Josh to a bedroom dominated by a queen-sized bed, and with a wardrobe, a stand which had a television and a Playstation, and a pedestal fan running. Sophie was as gorgeous as Josh had tried to describe.

"Sophie, this is my twin brother Glen."

"Hi Sophie."

"Hi Glen. Please sit."

They all sat on the big bed.

"I never realised twins could be so different-looking."

"There's a biological reason for that," Josh said, "but in many ways we're closer than normal brothers. We grew up together; we were in the same classes in school, same sporting teams...."

"Same everything," Glen said.

Josh laughed. "Yeah, until now."

"I'm at our old house and you're living here."

"That's right. What do you think?"

"It's good.  I'm glad you're happy."

"And now you have plans for your future," Josh said.

Josh knew about Glen but Glen didn't know about Josh, except living with Sophie and her family.

"You?" Glen asked.

"I'm still at Mitre 10 and also helping in Jack's business.  I get paid for that too."

"Ah."  Glen looked at Sophie.  "You're doing Year 12, Hannah tells me."

Sophie laughed.  "At least I have one friend at school!"

"After you finish school?"

"I'd like to do hairdressing," Sophie said while Josh looked at her out of the corners of his eyes.  Sophie had lovely hair: blonde and long to almost her waist.

"Josh?" Glen asked.

"I'm busy now but maybe something.  You're going to study business at the TAFE?"

"I plan to, but if I do I'll have to move to get a job.  Probably to Wagga."

"Wagga's nice," Sophie said.  "I come from there."

Josh frowned.  "If I give up Mitre 10 I can study."

"You should," Sophie said.

"I think I will," Josh said.  "Then we could move to Wagga for decent jobs."

"You'll like it there.  How about you study here, and I go to the TAFE the year after next."

"I have bad news," Glen said. "They don't offer hairdressing here, just salon assistant."

"That's a shame, no. Wagga TAFE will have the full range of courses. How about you carry on as now for next year, and then we move to Wagga the year after? We'll stay with my grandparents, get part-time jobs for spending money, and study at the TAFE there?"

Josh nodded his head. "Yes, we'll do that," he said. He looked to Glen. "Done."

"You're a good influence, Glen," Sophie said with a bright smile. Josh was right, Sophie was lovely. Bright and switched-on.

"You'll have to get used to being around twins," Glen said. "We're kind-of close."

"I'm an only child so it's been good for me to have a boyfriend, and I've met Hannah a few times so she's a friend now, and we'll be closer when we go to school I'm sure. Now I've got my boyfriend's brother so that's good for me too."

Glen was touched by that. Josh was right; Sophie was really lovely.

* * *

Josh was engrossed in playing mission 3 of Call of Duty: Modern Warfare against Sophie until he noticed his phone was ringing. He grabbed it from beside on their bed: Emma.

"Hi Emma," he greeted.

"Hi Josh. I'm after 10 points."

Big order. "That'll be 350."

"No problem."

"I'll bring it around in 20 minutes."

"Good."

She ended the call.

"Emma wants 10 points."

"That's a lot."

"She must be stocking up, I hope." Josh stood to slip on his runners. "Won't be long." Josh grabbed 10 bags before heading out to his car parked on the driveway. It wasn't far, only 10 minutes, when he parked out front of Emma's new unit. Josh pulled out his phone and rang the last called number.

"I'm outside," he said.

"Front door's unlocked."

Josh used a now familiar door to enter a familiar corridor and end up her living room. Josh handed the packets over while Emma rummaged through her bag. She pulled out a bundle of 20 and 50 dollar notes and counted them out while Josh watched. Josh put them in his pocket.

"That'll keep you going for a while," he said while thinking that was a lot of money from a girl who, to the best of his knowledge, still wasn't working much. He wondered how she paid for drugs and the rent for this unit.

"Do you want to – try one I guess?" Emma asked.

"No thanks Emma. You're my favourite customer but – you know."

"Say hello to Sophie for me."

"I will."

Josh headed out to his car to be home not so long after. He gave the money to Jack, who gave some of it back for rummaging through his wallet make up 85 dollars to Josh. Josh returned to their room where Sophie was cross-legged on the bed frowning at her phone. She looked up.

"I was curious so I searched Tinder for girls in Young, where I found 'Luscious Lucy' who you might recognise," as she handed the phone across.

Josh frowned as he scrolled her pictures, quite well done with her face hidden by her long hair although he knew her body well enough. He read her profile which implied good times, and no doubt fees were discussed when men who after good times contacted her.

"How did you recognise Emma? Josh asked.

"Emma has a tattoo on the back of her neck."

"The infinite knot: the infinite wisdom and compassion of Buddha for all sentient beings. She's into Buddhism so I gave her that tattoo for her birthday."

"She might be on sugar baby sites as well," Sophie said.

Josh handed the phone back. "It's her life," he said. "As far as I know she's not been able to find a job beyond a few hours a week, and she has no boyfriend."

"But still...."

"Who are we to judge?  I'm sure she's not the only one."

"You're right about that.  It's just a business for her I suppose.  In fact in a town like Young, word will get around like with us."

Indeed it would.

"Those 10 points," Sophie said, "she might not be stocking up.  Either her habit is spiralling out of control and she needs to work like that, or working like that is causing her habit to spiral."

Josh rubbed his chin while he thought.  "You might be right given she doesn't have much to do all day."

"So spiralling then working to pay for it?"

"Yeah."

"Common enough."

Sophie would know.  "Now where were we?" as Josh contemplated the paused game.

"Me beating you again," Sophie said as she moved to sit on the edge of her bed, controller in hand, ready to continue their game.

## Chapter Ten

Saturday morning in Young where Glen was sure the routine hadn't changed. After Mum and then Kev showered, Glen took his turn to shower and to shave too, before dressing. It was hot outside, not humid like Sydney but the sunlight was more intense. Apparently Sydney's perpetual smog filtered the sunlight there. Glen dressed in a t-shirt, shorts and runners before going to the kitchen where Mum and Kev both had mugs of coffee and both were smoking. Glen sighed: staying at home made sense economically, but staying there had its downsides. Apart from Sophie, Glen understood why Josh moved out, and in fact he moved out before he met Sophie. If Glen got a job while he studied he could move out too. At least for now he wasn't pressured but he would look for a suitable job after the Christmas break.

Glen switched on the kettle to make coffee, checked the cupboard but Mum only had white bread which wasn't healthy but would have to do. He toasted two slices to have with coffee, milk and sugar. Then he washed and put away his plates.

"Going out Mum," he said.

Mum said nothing as she stared into space while smoking another cigarette.

The Chinese Gardens weren't far and several cars were there. Glen saw a group on the banks of the lake in the shade of a gum tree. He went to James, Matt, Emma, Alana, Leah,

Noah, Lucas, Charlotte and Zoe. Justin and his boyfriend Toby weren't there.

"Hi all," Glen greeted.

"Hi Glen!" was the bright response from everyone.

Glen sat in the shade of the tree. "How are you all?" he asked.

"Getting by," James said. "Josh said you were coming home."

"Sydney's shit."

"Surely there's nightlife?"

"There's nightlife but there are traffic jams too, even at ten at night, even on Saturday night. Actually, Saturday night's are the worst. In any case just getting to what's happening makes it barely worthwhile."

"Really? Well, we have parties here most Saturday nights."

"Where are Justin and Toby?" Glen asked.

"Arranging their marriage."

Glen wasn't surprised about that. Those two were seriously in love.

"They had a great party for their engagement," Emma said. "Josh brightened it up."

"How?" Glen asked.

"He's dealing drugs now."

Glen was shocked. "Really?"

"Yeah, and it's good stuff too. The best. They do a lot of business."

93

"From where he lives?" Glen asked.

"Yes."

Glen couldn't believe that.

"Here they are now," Emma said.

Glen looked up to see Josh and Sophie, hand in hand; Sophie barely dressed like at her place the other afternoon, although she had the figure to carry that look. Drug dealing from home, probably Jack and Jessica and Sophie too. Amazing! No, wrong, too wrong.

"Hi," Josh said, echoed by Sophie before they sat. "Anything new happening, apart from Glen coming home?"

"I'm getting by," Emma said.

They talked about inanities but Glen's mind was far, far away. He had to stop this, this was wrong. But how? Talk with Josh when he had the chance.

"Are we still swimming?" Sophie asked.

"Yes we are," James said. "Do you want to go now? With the drought hardly any rivers or creeks are running, but Koorawatha Falls with the weir is fine."

"Under this I'm wearing a bikini!"

"And egg sandwiches and cordial in your car?"

Sophie smiled. "Those too."

Sophie had made herself at home with Josh's friends; she was particularly vivacious.

Sophie stood. "Let's go!"

94

"I'll stop at home to get my swimmers," Glen said, disappointed he couldn't talk with Josh. Maybe at Koorawatha Falls. They headed to the carpark to drive away as a type of convoy, with Glen taking a small detour but not really far out of the way.

* * *

Part-way along the road from Young to Cowra was the village of Koorawatha, with a faded sign pointing to Koorawatha Falls, four kilometres. After turning left, the bitumen road soon changed to dirt, but decent well-graded dirt amidst parched, dry fields and shaded by gum trees. Further along before a gate, a sign pointed to a track on the left, where the going was somewhat rougher but no problem as long as you slowed down. This track also crossed parched fields; the drought in New South Wales was terrible. Already bushfires were burning in the north of the state and it was sure to be a bad summer for fires. Across a narrow timber bridge, and just a bit further on was Koorawatha Falls, although no water was falling. Glen parked his car as the group stood in the shade of gum trees beside the lake formed by the weir. They'd changed with Sophie in a tiny bikini that mirrored the short, white shorts and the tiny top she wore before. A tiny bikini that covered what needed to be covered and no more.

"Let's go!" Sophie announced.

"Don't jump," Josh warned. "It'll be shallow."

"I know."

Instead she waded in followed by Josh, followed by the others with the girls in their swimmers somewhat more discreet than Sophie, but none of the girls had Sophie's figure, except Emma who had a fuller figure but was totally gorgeous. Glen took off his runners, t-shirt and shorts to reveal boxer swimmers, to wade into cool, somewhat muddy water, but delightful on an already hot day, especially shaded by many gum trees surrounding the lake beneath the falls.

"This is lovely," Sophie announced. "Skinny-dipping's wonderful, you know." Silence. "Anyone?"

"I will if you will," Emma said.

"Ha!"

In a flash Sophie untied her brief bikini top and tiny bikini bottom to put them on the bank, so Emma untied her top and pulled off her bikini bottom to put them on the bank too.

"Come on!" Sophie said to Josh. "You've skinny-dipped before I'm sure. Probably here."

They had indeed. Josh removed his bathers, he had a good figure and better than the other guys.

"Glen?" Sophie asked.

Sophie was right, skinny-dipping was wonderful. Glen took his bathers off and it felt great! Even though bathers were tiny, water caressing you all over was sublimely incredible. More outfits were shed until all of the group were naked in the water, laughing and splashing. Glen really, really understood why Josh said he loved Sophie; she was amazing.

96

Josh must totally love her. They laughed, joked and played for ages.

"If we were naked all the time," Sophie said. "The world would be a better place."

"The world would be completely uninhibited," Emma said.

"Doesn't being naked feel like a special bonding? You're all close friends, I know this, but at this moment you're closer?"

She was right. "Yes," Glen said. "It's odd, I can't explain it, but yes."

"We ought to have lunch now," Josh said.

"Like this?" Sophie asked.

"If you want."

That was a step further but why not? Glen had a bottle of water but he didn't have lunch.

"I must have known you were coming, Glen, because I made more than usual," Sophie said. "You can have some cordial too."

"Which cordial is it?" Josh asked.

"Lemon, lime and bitters."

"Have some," Josh offered.

"Thanks."

They climbed out to the dusty, barely grassed bank where Sophie went to their car to fetch a bag. In it was a container of sandwiches, a glass bottle of drink and two plastic cups. Glen thought.

"I'll fetch a bottle for some of your drink."

Glen did, to have it part-filled with lemon, lime and bitters, and to be given a scrambled egg sandwich.

"Sophie likes eggs," Josh said flatly. "Cordial and eggs, not that I'm complaining."

"You better not complain," she said with a bright smile.

Glen felt a warm glow; Sophie's comment about nakedness and bonding was true because he felt particularly close to her now. Close all his friends eating lunch in a big naked group.

"Emma told me about your business," Glen said.

"Are you shocked?" Josh asked.

"Is it right?"

"Every customer has come from Daniel or Mike. If it wasn't us it would be either of those two."

"But..."

"But nothing, Glen. The war on drugs has never worked and never will work. Not only that but the worst drug is alcohol. How many women have been beaten up and even killed because of alcohol? And guys? Nightclubs in Sydney still close early because of drunken fights. Cocaine or heroin of MDMA doesn't do that. Tell me I'm wrong?"

Glen couldn't. "You're right about both. Users use drugs no matter who's selling, and alcohol is our biggest problem."

"Even ice is alright unless you get addicted. Then you can get violent when you're coming down, but most don't get that far."

"What if you're caught?"

"For a first time, a CCO or something like that," Sophie said.

"And you, Sophie?" Glen asked.

"At the moment we're selling and making money that way, but in the longer-term you know what I want to do."

"You know my plan is to move to Wagga the year after next and probably study business like you," Josh said. "Don't tell Mum or Hannah what we're doing now, although I don't think Mum will care. She hates Sophie. I don't know why."

Glen knew "It's because you're happy and she's never been happy," he said.

Josh nodded his head. "Yeah, you're right."

"Is that right?" Sophie asked.

"It's not you, it's her," Josh said.

"I'm sorry for your Mum if that's been her life."

"Thinking it through I'm sorry for her too, but she's never going to change so we have to pretend she doesn't exist. It's sad, but for our protection we have to."

"Josh is right; keep away from her," Glen said. "One day I'll have to do the same."

They finished eating and drinking so Sophie packed up and put it in the car. Glen felt calmer now.

"Come on everyone!" Sophie called. "One last swim!"

She tore into the water followed by naked everyone.

"Come on Glen," Josh said as he stood. "One thing about Sophie is she gets what she wants."

Josh raced to the water shouting while Glen did the same. Soon it was laughter, water fights and dunking again. What a great way to spend a hot, sunny, Saturday afternoon.

## Chapter Eleven

The laundry door opening to the backyard was where the action was, so Jack installed a battery-powered buzzer. It started slowly, one or two a day, but as weeks passed to months they gradually built to a steady stream. Josh's contacts contacted others who contacted others who contacted others. Sophie arranged for Josh to be given one-quarter of everything, given almost all their business came from Josh directly or indirectly. In exchange Josh offered to pay one-quarter of Jack and Jessica's rent, one quarter of other bills like water, gas and electricity, and one-quarter of household groceries. Now that she had a live-in boyfriend it appeared that Sophie cooked more than before, breakfasts and lunches, and the two women took turns cooking dinner, but mostly Jessica. Sometimes Josh did deliveries, and there were parties most Saturday nights where business could be made and fun could be had. Josh continued with Mitre 10 to give himself something to do, especially as Sophie started school next week and Josh didn't want to be home all day, every day just with Jack and Jessica.

Sophie came into their room carrying her Wagga Wagga High School backpack and a couple of white blouses draped over her arm.

"The uniform here...," she muttered. She looked to Josh. "Skirts have to be knee length, or there are long, baggy shorts like my Grandma would wear. So I decided to wear slacks summer and winter. Mum sewed new logos on my old blouses. Here, I'll show you and you can tell me what you think."

Josh knew he could only tell Sophie, no matter how she looked, that she looked good while she removed tight jeans and a halter top, to replace them with a white blouse which had a Young High School logo on the top pocket, and plain, blue slacks not particularly tight. Then white socks and black shoes.

"How do I look?"

"You look good."

"Honestly?"

Josh couldn't help but smile. "Honestly. I know if you chose slacks they would be tighter, but those slacks are fine. I can still see your cute bottom."

"Really?"

"Really. You have to meet their requirements but you picked the best look from the list. I know from when I was at school their knee-length skirts or baggy shorts are terrible, but those slacks are good. Your blouse is nice and your shoes are oddly sexy."

"Sexy?"

"Sexy like the way boots are sexy."

"My blouse and shoes are from Wagga. In Wagga we could wear shorter skirts, which I did in summer."

"Looking forward to school?" Josh asked.

"I'm sure it's going to be busy."

"Intense is a better word."

"You'll help me?"

"I can help you now to prepare, if you want."

"Let me change, no, I'll stay as I am so I'm in a student mood."

Josh knew he was going to miss Sophie when she went to school, rather than lying in every morning then having breakfast together, playing games whenever they wanted to, sex whenever they wanted to, going skinny-dipping at Koorawatha Falls together, and all the other things they did. But even with school they still would have special times, like lying in on weekends followed by breakfast, Saturdays with his friends who were Sophie's friends now, and there would always be time for sex. Josh realised his thoughts were straying so he focussed on advice to get Sophie ready for what would be the most important ten months of her life. For sure Josh could help and Sophie would be better prepared for year 12 than he was. In fact Josh and Glen both became almost overwhelmed before they came to grips with what was expected. Josh thought about where to start.

## Chapter Twelve

Daniel wheeled his BMW into the Caltex in the carpark of the Woolworths supermarket to pull up beside the diesel pump. There he removed the cap to put the nozzle, always greasy, to fill his thirsty beast. On and on and on till the pump clicked off. He glanced at the pump: 72 litres and 112.96. He went inside before looking outside for his pump number. Then Daniel realised he didn't have cash so would have to use his card.

"Pump number two," Daniel said to the middle-aged female casher.

"That'll be 112 dollars 96."

Daniel tapped his Visa debit card, keyed the pin because it was more than 100 dollars, and waited.

"Declined, insufficient funds," the cashier said flatly.

"What?" No. Fortunately they took AMEX so he tapped that and keyed the pin.

"Receipt?" she asked.

Daniel kept them for his 'business'. "Yes," he said.

Back into the BMW and home, where he parked it in the driveway as usual. He ought to clean the junk out of the garage. In through the back door.

"Lisa!" Daniel called. "Where's all our money?"

"Why?" she asked.

"I tried to use the debit card to fill the BMW but it was declined, insufficient funds."

"You should know."

"Know what?" Daniel asked.

"Sales are down these past weeks."

"So?"

"The money you give me covers groceries and bills but there's not enough to top up the account. So there's nothing there."

"How much cash do we have?"

"I had to pay Franco yesterday so I've got a couple of hundred."

"That's all?"

"You're only selling to three or four customers a day, if that."

Daniel then realised Lisa was right; business was down. He hadn't seen many regulars for a long time.

"It must be that new dealer: Jack Bishop," Lisa said.

"Must be," Daniel said. "How the fuck did he hit our business so hard in two months?"

"He's got Josh Ward working for him. Actually living with him."

"So how much do you reckon we're down?"

"We've lost about half. If you hadn't bought that BWW...."

"It was a special deal."

"But still, 130,000."

Actually more than that once Daniel paid on-road costs! Regardless of that, Daniel knew he needed help.

"I'm going out," he said.

Into the BMW to drive to Mike. Soon he was sitting out the back of Mike's house under their pergola with a tinted Perspex roof, with stubbies each.

"Jack Bishop...," Daniel said.

"Yeah, fuck him."

"You too?"

"Down about a third."

"About half for me."

"Franco's going to be pissed-off big time."

"For sure," Mike said before he drank some beer.

"Any ideas?" Daniel asked

"Fucked if I know. Apparently it's good stuff, better than Franco's, and cheaper although I'm sure he'll put his prices up soon enough."

"Who's his supplier?" Daniel asked.

"Don't know. Franco might know. Bishop comes from Wagga."

Daniel drank while thinking.

"I ought to ring Franco," Daniel said.

"Good idea."

"I'll do it now."

Daniel pulled out his iPhone to press Franco's contact.

"Daniel," Franco said abruptly.

"What do you know about Jack Bishop?"

"Local dealer associated with a bikie group: Devil's Ride."

"He's living here now and making a nuisance of himself."

"How big a nuisance?"

"Quite big. He's hurting us."

"How?"

"Got a local guy working for him which would give him an in to local users, and apparently his stuff is good."

"So...?"

"Got any ideas?"

"Yeah I do. Get hold of a car, an anonymous car that isn't either of your cars and not that BMW, get a shotgun, get your families out of your houses one evening, and do a drive-by on your own houses. The police will do the rest."

Daniel frowned while he thought. Bikie gangs were synonymous with drive-by shootings so that would work.

"Got any ideas where to get a shotgun?" Daniel asked

"Fuck Daniel!"

Daniel then remembered his father had rifles. "I know someone," he said.

"Good. I know I don't have to say to with the police investigating a drive-by, you should clear all product out of your houses."

Daniel hadn't thought of that. "Of course Franco," he said

"So I'll see it on the Riverina news one evening?"

"Yes you will."

Franco ended the call.

Daniel looked to Mike "We'll do drive-by shootings on our own houses," Daniel said. "That will point the police towards Jack Bishop."

"That sounds like a plan," Mike said, before he drank more beer.

* * *

Daniel pulled up at his parents place just out Canowindra, north of Cowra. A pissy little town of about 2,000 people where nothing changed and virtually nothing happened. His parents had a farm of 2,000 acres normally grazing sheep, except their paddocks were bare and they were buying fodder to keep their breeding stock alive. Daniel kept them afloat with a loan he knew wouldn't be repaid. He rang the buzzer to be greeted by Mum.

"Hello Daniel," she said. "This is a surprise."

"Dad at home?"

"He's in the shed."

Daniel crossed a dry and dusty yard; they desperately needed rain, where Dad was in the big, open shed pouring oil into the engine of the big tractor.

"Hi Dad."

"Hi Daniel."

"I'm here to see if you can help me. I've got a mate coming from the UK to stay with us for a while, and I thought we'd do a bit of target shooting which is something they can't easily do over there. I remember you have a couple of shotguns from when duck hunting was legal."

"Yeah, I do, but it's been ages since they were used."

"Do they work?"

"They've been stored properly so they'll be fine."

"Can I borrow one for a few days?"

"Can't see why not. This isn't your business?" Dad then frowned.

"No, no; just fun."

"Alright, come with me."

They went into the house where Dad grabbed the key for the gun locker. There he had a fair collection, shooting rabbits and foxes were a necessity on a farm rather than a sport, and two shotguns. He took them out.

"Pellets are in there."

Daniel reached in for two heavy cardboard boxes.

"We'll take them to your car."

Daniel followed his father to the BMW where the guns and pallets were placed in the back.

"Be careful with those," Dad said.

"I've been handling them since – how long?"

"You've been shooting since you were young."

"See ya Dad."

"Bye Daniel."

Daniel drove along their dry, dirt driveway to O'Briens Road; then turned towards Canowindra. From there he picked up the highway to Cowra and further to Young. Straight to Mike's place. As soon as Daniel pulled up on Mike's driveway, Mike came from the back of his house.

"You've got a shotgun?" he asked.

"Yeah I have," Daniel said. "You got the car?"

"It's near the storage units."

"Cleaned out your product?"

"To my storage unit. You?"

"The same." Daniel looked towards the fading sun. "About this time tomorrow night. Get Zoe out of the house, I'll tell Lisa and the kids, and then we do it. My place then your place."

"Too easy!"

Daniel climbed into the BMW to drive home. Too easy — just get families out of two houses and do it.

## Chapter Thirteen

Josh sat on the bonnet of his car parked outside Young High School as a massive crowd of students, all dressed in white and blue uniforms, surged out of the gate. The older students, recognisably taller, walked rather than ran. Josh remembered as the years ticked by at school you and became more like an adult. Josh spotted Sophie with Hannah and three other girls. He strolled to them.

"Hi Sophie, hi Hannah."

"Hi Josh," they echoed.

"How was your day?" Josh asked Sophie.

"Busy with new subjects and meeting new teachers, and being warned about what was coming although I knew that already, and just settling down." Sophie looked to the other girls. "See you tomorrow."

"See you," was the universal goodbye.

Josh walked with Sophie to his car.

"You didn't have to pick me up," she said.

"Are you embarrassed?"

"Hardly! Actually it's good you did. A couple of guys tried to flirt with me but now they know I've got an older boyfriend."

Josh climbed in while Sophie put her backpack on the backseat before climbing in and buckling up.

"They were just boys," Sophie said. "Girls grow up quicker, so you and me fit well that way."

"How old are you?"

"I'll be 17 in March. You?"

"I turned 19 in October."

Josh started his car and drove away with Sophie beside him looking deep in thought. She put her hand on his heart. "I know I'm here, unlike someone I knew before."

Josh drove home, to follow Sophie inside where it was hot, although their fan made their room bearable. Sophie dumped her bag in the corner then set to changing except Josh grabbed her arm.

"Later, soon, things will get busy with assignments, as you can imagine."

She smiled. "Yeah, alright. I'll shower to freshen up." Josh watched her take a halter top and shorts from the wardrobe although she wouldn't be wearing those for long.

* * *

Jack always had a beer with his evening meal, while Josh sometimes had a cider but mostly he had cordial. Beyond that, Jack couldn't hide his smirk while Josh tried to hold as straight a face as he could manage. Sophie brought in two lemon cordials.

"Cheers," Jack said before taking a swig of his stubby.

"Cheers," Josh and Sophie echoed before swigs of lemon cordial.

Jessica entered carrying two plates of spaghetti bolognaise, as Sophie dashed out to grab two more plates and Jessica then brought a salad. They ate.

"How was school?" Jessica asked.

"Good, fine," Sophie said. "No. I have a plan as you know so I'm going to do the best I can to reach my goals."

"You're growing up, Sophie; I'm proud of you."

"Thanks Mum."

"Josh has a plan too."

Josh thought. "Girls grow up quicker," he said. "I'm now in step with Sophie."

Jessica nodded her head. "You're right about growing up quicker," she eventually said.

"How about my real dad?" Sophie asked. "What was he like?"

"Don't even think about him," Jessica said. "Your dad is your real dad in all ways except one, and Jack loves you like a daughter so you have two dads. Don't think about that other guy – please."

"I'm a bit curious, but alright."

Josh pondered that. Jessica was 32 now, so she was 15 or 16 when she fell pregnant, and seemed to have later met and married the man who Sophie called Dad. Interesting. That other guy might not have been consensual.

Suddenly police sirens shattered a quiet Tuesday evening. More and more and more and ambulances too. Josh stopped eating as did everyone.

"Young has become like Sydney," Jack said.

"What do you think?" Sophie asked.

"A long, hot night, too much beer, a domestic."

"Murder?"

"Who knows? Possibly."

"That's awful."

"It is."

"A good man who treats women with respect is worth more than all the – I don't know," Jessica said. "Worth more than I can describe," she said as she put her hand on Jack's big hand.

Sophie put her hand on Josh's slim hand while looking at him with – something. With love in her eyes. She squeezed his hand before returning to eating.

* * *

Jack was always up early and always listened to the 8am news bulletin on ABC radio. An inland New South Wales tradition, in fact. These days Josh was up early so he sat with Jack in the kitchen just on eight, where the lead story was two drive-by shootings in Young last evening, thought to be from the same perpetrators, with property damage at two houses and no casualties. Young CIB Detective-Sergeant McDonald said investigations were ongoing. Jack switched off the small, rather old-fashioned transistor radio while Josh looked to Jessica leaning against the doorframe while she smoked a cigarette.

"What do you think?" Jessica asked before drawing on her cigarette.

Jack frowned deeply. "That's interesting," he eventually said.

"Where those drive-bys Trev and his mates from Devil's Ride?"

"No, definitely not. Last time we spoke, Trev was more than happy with the progress we've made here. In fact something like this might create trouble for us. If the police suspect us they'll come knocking. We need to get this place clean, now. Everything to the storage unit."

"Do you think the two properties are Daniel Stewart and Mike Kelly?" Jessica asked.

"I don't know but we'll assume they are."

"What about customers?" Josh asked.

"Deliveries via the storage unit for those who ring, and if they come here we'll drive them to the storage unit and then back here. You're an ex-customer; would that have worked for you?"

"Yeah, it would have," Josh said.

"Wait for Sophie to leave for school," Jessica said, "so we don't upset her when she needs to be concentrating."

Josh agreed with that while Jessica butted her cigarette.

"Fuck, there's always something," she muttered to herself before heading off.

"When we clean up, Josh," Jack said. "That means personal supplies in your room."

"We don't do much but I'll double-check."

"How much do you do?"

"We have a routine of Friday nights once a fortnight, after I get paid at Mitre 10. You?"

"Maybe every few weeks like you," he said. "Just a treat."

"It's a nice treat."

"Better that than binge drinking or sexting or whatever kids do these days." Jack smiled brightly. "Sophie doesn't need to sext you; you've got the real thing!" and he laughed.

"Sophie's special like her mother's special," Josh said.

"Yeah, you're right, they're both great."

"Are you talking about me?" Sophie asked before pouring a bowl of her favourite Nutri Grain breakfast cereal and then filling it with milk. She leaned against the doorway to eat.

"We might be," Josh said.

"Like mother like daughter, in all the good ways," Jack said.

"Do you think so?"

"In all the good ways," Josh echoed.

"I'll head off to school now," Sophie said as she put her bowl in the sink. "What was it with the police and ambulances last night?"

116

"Two drive-by shootings," Jack said while Josh glanced to him before realising Sophie would hear about that at school soon enough.

"Alright, see you both."

"See you Sophie," Jack said.

"See you my love," Josh said.

"Ha!"

She headed out.

"Women have it easy," Jack said. "They're intrinsically beautiful and wonderful."

"No, women don't have it easy," Josh said. "Sophie's gorgeous, the most beautiful girl in the world, but she's fixated that her bust is too small. I tell her she's fine and I like her bust, but that doesn't change the way she feels. My ex has a naturally full figure and is totally gorgeous, but she was borderline depressed particularly about her legs!"

"Jessica is worried about her bust too."

"What about my bust?" Jessica asked.

"Your bust is just right for me. You know girls with nice bottoms have smaller busts and the other way around."

"Is that right?" Jessica asked.

"Give me your arse any day!"

"I'll tell Sophie that," Josh said.

"Do."

"That's my daughter you're talking about," Jessica said.

"I love her."

117

"I know."

Jack stood. "Lets clean this place up, and if the police call we were eating; what was it?"

"Spaghetti bolognaise with a green salad," Jessica said.

"That's right."

Jack headed off while Josh hoped he hadn't found himself in the middle of a drug war.

## Chapter Fourteen

As Luke pulled on his uniform, followed by his vest, baton and pistol, he heard the buzz from the Operations Room. There Young CIB: Detective-Sergeant Keith McDonald and Detective-Constable Ron Jackson, as well as Acting Inspector Kevin Rogers, were in earnest conversation with Leon; officially Senior Sergeant Leon Fowler.

"Ah, Senior Constable Scott," Inspector Rogers said. "Just the man we need. Yesterday evening as you're probably aware, there were two drive-by shootings at houses occupied by Daniel Stewart, Mike Kelly and their families. Fortunately nobody was injured. I know Stewart and Kelly are suspected of dealing drugs, is there anything else you know of?"

There was. "Rumour has it that Jack Bishop recently moved from Wagga Wagga to here to deal drugs," Luke said. "Bishop is reported to be friends with Trevor Davies of the Devil's Ride Motorcycle Gang, based in Sydney."

"There's the answer!" Detective-Sergeant McDonald exclaimed.

"Not exactly," Luke said. "Being new in town, it wouldn't make a lot of sense for Bishop to create a scene and get us involved. This can only be bad for his business."

"You're uniform branch and we're detectives."

"Alright," Luke said, even though it wasn't alright; more that he had no choice.

119

"I say we search Bishop's place now and bring everyone there for questioning," McDonald said.

"Excellent idea," Inspector Rogers agreed. "Senior Constable; do you know who lives there?"

"Beyond Jack Bishop, no."

For a search and arresting a number of suspects, we'll need the two of us from CIB and you two, Scott and Hewson. I'll get a search warrant from Magistrate Armstrong and meet you there."

"Well let's go!" Detective-Sergeant McDonald exclaimed. "Where?"

Luke pulled out his notebook to scroll pages. "Bishop lives at 37 Blackett Street."

"Let's go!"

They headed out the door with Luke and Alice trailing.

"Do you need a degree in stupid to be promoted to detective?" Luke asked quietly.

"Luke!"

"We won't find anything because Bishop's not involved."

"His supplier, the bikie gang, might have done it?"

"Even if the bikie gang did this, searching Bishop's house and interrogating Bishop won't discover that."

Luke and Alice reached car 313, to climb in and follow the detectives' unmarked white Holden Commodore to 37 Blackett Street, where they waited for Inspector Rogers to arrive holding the precious search warrant. Luke and Alice were asked to go to the back door in case anyone tried to escape. After heavy knocking and shouting 'police', Luke and Alice were let inside the little, fibro house. By then McDonald had gathered all occupants into the living room: an older man, a woman in her 30s, a teenage girl, and local boy Joshua Ward. Names were taken and recorded by Detective-Constable Jackson: Jack Bishop, Jessica Weaver, Sophie Weaver, and Josh Ward. In the background, watching but not participating, stood Inspector Rogers.

"Well, search," Detective-Sergeant McDonald ordered.

"Be careful with their belongings," Luke whispered to Alice.

With latex gloves they carefully searched that little house, for nothing of course. McDonald scratched his chin. "Roof space," he eventually said.

"Garage," Alice offered.

"That too."

It was agreed the two detectives would search the garage, while Alice got the torch from their car and Luke took a step ladder from the garage to climb into the roof cavity, where with that torch there was nothing more than furnace-like heat. He climbed down."

"Is that all?" Alice asked.

"Nothing there," Luke said.

Back in the living room, Detective-Sergeant McDonald literally scratched his head. "Alright," he said. "We would like to interview you all at Young Police Station."

"What for?" Jessica Weaver asked.

"To ascertain your involvement in last night's drive-by shootings."

"We had no involvement."

"Then your interviews will be straightforward."

"It's alright Jessica," Jack Bishop said. "We agree to be interviewed."

"Adults with us," McDonald said. "The younger two with Scott and Hewson."

Alice escorted Sophie Weaver and Josh Ward to the back of their car. Luke got ready for the short drive to Young Police Station.

* * *

Josh and Sophie were escorted inside the police station, through a door with a one-way window to one side. Sophie was told to wait on a padded bench in the corridor while Josh was taken into a small, windowless room with a table and two plastic chairs on either side; chairs a lot like the dining chairs at Blackett Street. On the table was a tape recorder of some type. Josh was gestured to sit before the two police officers sat opposite.

Senior Constable Hewson then pressed an old tape recorder key; actually two keys simultaneously.

"My name's Senior Constable Luke Scott and with me is Constable Alice Hewson. Joshua Ward; I've been told to ask you questions on the record, and as such you're entitled to have a lawyer present if you so desire. If you can't afford a lawyer, one will be appointed free of charge to you. Do you understand?"

"I understand," Josh said but he knew he was fine. They didn't do these drive-by shootings nor did Jack's supplier, the bikie gang. The police search revealed nothing incriminating, of course.

"Do you know anything about the drive-by shootings against two premises yesterday evening at 6 15 and 6 25?" he asked.

"I was eating dinner with Jack, Jessica and Sophie when we heard police and ambulance sirens. Jack thought it was domestic violence."

"Can anyone outside the household verify this?"

"No."

"Do you believe the Devil's Ride bikie gang was involved?"

"You'll have to ask them."

"Do you have anything else to say?"

"No, sorry."

The senior constable flicked the tape recorder off, to the surprise of Josh.

"Alright Josh; you're free to go."

Josh left to wait on the padded bench in the corridor while they interviewed Sophie, which took all of two or three minutes. Josh and Sophie were led to the pubic area of the police station to wait for Jack and Jessica whose interviews ran for longer. Eventually they gathered in the carpark. Being interviewed was no problem but their car rides were only one-way which wasn't fair. After catching a taxi home they gathered in the living room.

"How did it go?" Jessica asked Sophie.

"The two police constables, Luke Scott and Alice Hewson, didn't take my interview seriously."

"They didn't take it seriously with me," Josh said.

"At least two police here have brains," Jessica said. "I think this is over as far as we're concerned."

"I wonder who did it, and why," Josh said.

"Interesting question," Jack said.

It was indeed.

## Chapter Fifteen

Daniel heard the front door buzzer.

"I'll get it!" Lisa shouted. Moments later, "G'day Mike, come in."

Daniel went to the entrance hall. "G'day mate," he offered.

"G'day. Kid's home?"

"They're at playgroup," Lisa said. "Come inside."

They went into a living room where heat was moderated by their whole-house evaporative cooler.

"Word has it that CIB detectives paid a visit to Jack Bishop but found nothing," Mike said.

"No!" Daniel exclaimed.

"Bishop has thought two drive-bys, bikie gangs do drive-bys like the police thought, my supplier's a bikie gang, I better prepare," Lisa said.

"So we got nowhere?" Daniel asked.

"Well you got somewhere," Lisa said. "Now Bishop will be after you two and Franco's still going to be pissed that you let Bishop steal half his business."

"Any ideas?"

"Better quality, cheaper prices, and hope that brings your customers back. From what I've sold you've lost most of your younger customers."

"Lisa's right," Mike said.

125

"That's down to Josh Ward," Lisa said. "Not only Josh; his girlfriend, Bishop's partner's girl, has made herself part of the scene here. Every Saturday night."

"That's why I'm not selling any E."

"Josh and his girlfriend have that sewn up. Not just party drugs, a lot of casual users are late teens and twenties."

"Back to square one and let's hope Bishop doesn't take it out on us," Daniel said.

"Nobody brings in police to solve disputes, but you two effectively did that with your fake drive-bys," Lisa said. "Look, I better pick the kids up. See ya later, Mike."

"See ya, Lisa."

"Take a seat and I'll get you a beer," Daniel said.

Daniel grabbed two cans from the fridge; gave one to Mike, pulled the ring-pull on his before sitting and thinking. "There's truth in what Lisa said," he said. "Better quality and cheaper prices, and hope that brings customers back." He drank.

"What we've got are three dealers now when before there were two. Franco will just have to deal with that." Mike pulled his ring-pull and drank too.

"Better idea!" Daniel said. "Put the onus back on Franco. He has to come up with quality to match Bishop's supplier."

"Next time Franco complains about business, I'll tell him that."

"Both of us, mate, both of us."

126

Daniel drank more of his beer while thinking Franco was only part of his problem. His bigger problem was the house loan, the car loan, and barely enough cash coming in to pay their bills after he paid those two. Waiting for Franco to fix his end, which wasn't going to happen given Franco bought from someone else, wouldn't help Daniel with his financial problems now. Daniel drank more beer. *Fuck Jack Bishop, Bishop's partner, Bishop's partner's girl and Josh! Fuck them all!*

## Chapter Sixteen

Josh held Sophie's cute bottom as he watched her caressing between her legs; so pretty with sparse, blonde hair. Josh's fucking mirrored Sophie's caresses; slow and steady, no hurry at all. Beautiful. Sophie looked down to Josh and smiled while still gently stroking herself. Josh closed his eyes to enjoy the sensation of it, to then watch Sophie, brow furrowed as she rubbed herself with more purpose. Josh dug his fingers into her bottom to fuck her with the same purpose while he felt sweet inside. Sophie, eyes closed, rubbing and rubbing, harder and harder, while Josh mirrored her harder and harder. Sophie rubbed and rubbed and rubbed while Josh felt himself close. Sophie gasped and clamped on Josh which tipped him over the edge. Pleasure and pleasure until it faded and he realised that he was still gripping her cute bottom so hard. The whole thing – incredible.

"Fuck yeah!" Sophie exclaimed which caused Josh to chuckle.

Sophie bent down to kiss Josh just as there was knocking on their door, before it opened wide and Jessica poked her head in.

"Oh, sorry!" before the door closed to a small gap. "Jack wants to talk," Jessica then said.

"Be there in a minute Mum!" Sophie called before laughing.

She climbed off, grabbed discarded panties to wipe down her leg; shrugged her shoulders before pulling on tiny denim shorts and a halter top, while Josh dressed in underwear first, then a t-shirt and shorts. They went to the living room where Jessica was by the open window, smoking. Sophie went to her.

Josh overheard Sophie whisper: "Next time Mum, knock and wait."

"I thought you would be busy with your homework," Jessica replied and then smoked more.

"There's always time for half an hour."

"Alright."

Jack was in an armchair with a stubby of beer.

"Our supplier is worried about the shooting the other evening," Jack said. "He'll be here soon."

Just then Josh heard the knocker. Jack left for the front door while Josh glanced out the window at a black BMW X5, the mirror image of Daniel's SUV, with three big guys in dark t-shirts and jeans standing around. Bikie gangs had moved beyond riding actual motorcycles. Jack escorted another big guy, 30s, in a black, Harley-Davidson t-shirt and jeans, with tattoos all over both arms. He smiled with a couple of missing teeth.

"Hello Trev," Jessica greeted.

"Hi Jessica." He went to Josh. "I'm Trev," as he put his hand out.

"Josh," as Josh shook hands.

Then to Sophie. "Does she need to be here?"

"Sophie is equal in this," Jack said firmly.

They shook hands in silence.

"What can you tell me about Daniel Stewart and Mike Kelly?"

Silence for a moment.

"Daniel's in his 30s," Josh said. "He has a partner Lisa and two daughters, an expensive house and an expensive car. I imagine he's lost business over the last two months."

"Mike Kelly?"

"I don't know him as well, but he's in his 30s with a partner Zoe who's pregnant. Daniel Stewart and Mike Kelly are friends."

"Rivals but friends?"

"Yeah."

"Could they have done this together?"

"Daniel's not the sharpest tool in the shed, but yeah, they could have."

"Don't do anything that's going to make things worse," Jack said. "This is a small town, not Sydney."

"I know. Have you done anything dodgy to upset them?"

"Nothing dodgy," Josh said. "Samples to friends and people I know, and their families and friends. They told me your stuff is good and the price is right. This is a small town like Jack said and word got around."

"Josh, can you show me to Stewart and Kelly?  We'll tell them we don't want any more trouble."

Josh froze while he thought about what to say.  "This is a small town, Trev.  The police here know who and what if things get out of hand."

"Just a chat and a promise there won't be more trouble."

Josh looked to Jack who nodded his head.

"Alright Trev," Josh said.  "Now?"

"Being a small town they know you're involved?" Trev asked Josh.

"I'm certain of it and Sophie too.  Sophie helps with parties on Saturday nights."

Trev nodded his head slowly.  "I see," he said slowly. "Come on Josh; let's sort this out peacefully."

Josh followed Trev to get into a seat of luscious leather while three bikies were squashed in the back, despite it being a big SUV.  They were big enough to scare the shit out of Daniel and Mike.

"Which way Josh?" Trev asked.

"Daniel Stewart first," Josh said.  "Down the end of this street and turn left."

Trev reversed the big, plush SUV out of the driveway to follow Josh's directions to 18 Matthew Street: an almost new, sprawling, four bedroom, three bathroom, two car garage house.  Josh guessed it was worth maybe 600,000 which was expensive for Young, although the two, three and four and even five hectare properties on the outskirts were worth well over a million.

"Is this it?" Trev asked.

"This is it," Josh said. "He does his deals around the back."

"Alright; let's deal with Daniel Stewart. You stay here, Josh."

Josh watched them stomp past a front yard of lush lawn with rock borders, volcanic rock and strange-looking tall shrubs or short trees, to the front door to hammer loudly. The door opened, before four, big, darkly-dressed bikies surged into the house. The door closed. About 20 minutes later the door opened and they strolled to the SUV. Trev slipped into the driver's seat.

"Done. Mike Kelly?"

Josh directed Trev to 3 Brocade Place, a decent but older, smaller, brick veneer house. There four bikies crossed a garden of parched grass and bare spots, beyond which was a paved area with a few bedraggled shrubs. The metal-framed mesh security door was hammered with a big fist, once more the front door was opened, and this time a flimsy security door that wasn't at all secure, was unlocked. Once more big bikies surged into a house, but only for several minutes. They returned where Trev once more slid into the driver's seat.

"Less argumentative," Trev said. "We're staying overnight at the Colonial Motel. Any ideas for a good time?"

"The best restaurant in town is the Mandarin Court, just walking distance from where you're staying."

"No, a proper good time mate!"

"Oh!" Josh exclaimed then thought - maybe. "This is a small town Trev."

"So you keep saying."

"So anyone I tell you about...."

"We're here for a good time."

Josh hoped he was doing the right thing. "There's Lucy if she's interested."

"Is she nice?"

"I'm sure she will be." Josh took his phone out to find Emma's number. "0412 777 937"

"Say that again," as Trev now had his phone in his big hand.

"0412 777 937"

"We'll drop you home and give Lucy a ring."

Once more Josh gave directions, this time to a fibro house far less luxurious than Daniel Stewart and Mike Kelly, but full of love. Josh climbed out while Trev's window glided down.

"Thanks for everything, Josh. Tell Jack he should be fine now."

"See you Trev."

"See ya Josh."

Josh went inside while hoping he'd done the right thing.

* * *

133

Daniel sat in the leather armchair in his living room, drinking a beer. For once the kids were quiet; those bikies put the fear of God into everyone! Lisa came in to stand over him.

"You were lucky, Daniel," she said with her arms crossed. "I hope you've learned your lesson."

Daniel stared into space. "Yeah I have," he said.

"Another stunt like those drive-bys and they'll put you in hospital."

That was for sure but that didn't solve Daniel's financial crisis. If he sold his BMW he would lose tens of thousands but maybe he didn't have a choice. But even if he sold it he still had his house payments. Daniel sighed as he sipped his beer.

\* \* \*

Emma's personal phone rang with a private number.

"Hello?" she answered.

"Is this Lucy?"

Ah, word of mouth. "Yes, I'm Lucy."

"My name's Trev; Josh told me about you."

Emma's heart skipped a beat and she suddenly felt sweaty. *Fuck!*

"Josh said you might be interested," Trev said.

Too late, Josh knew, and work was work. "I'm free," she said. "I have my own unit."

"Do you do outcalls?"

"Yes I do."

134

"We're staying in two apartments at the Colonial Motel."

*We're - plural?*

"There are four of us," Trev then said.

Emma needed clarification. "One at a time or all together?"

"All together for a few hours."

Emma charged 150 for a half-hour or 200 for an hour. She knew from her research that the charge for multiples was for each man. "That'll be 300 each for two hours."

"I don't like condoms."

Most didn't.

"Sorry Trev."

"Fifty?"

Emma stayed silent.

"One-hundred?"

"Alright."

"Anal?"

"An extra fifty."

"Good. When can you be here?"

"I can be there in half an hour."

"Meet us in apartment C."

He ended the call while Emma realised her hands were shaking. But still, 450 times four; 1,800 – fuck! Emma didn't want Josh to know but then Young was a small place. Sophie would know too but that hadn't changed her – but of course they dealt drugs! Emma went to shower, and while

135

showering she wondered. Since she'd been working Emma realised guys thought she was more than just alright: her breasts she thought were too big guys liked a lot, mostly they couldn't keep their hands off them, and her legs she thought were too thick guys really liked too. The older and married men and younger guys like James too, who didn't realise who Lucy was until he showed up. Emma dried herself before selecting a black g-string, a leather mini skirt, the top from her black bikini, and black stiletto sandals. With her hands still shaking she went to her old Toyota shaded in the carport. She slid behind the wheel and reversed out.

* * *

Everyone knew everywhere in Young, including the Colonial Motel just a block from Boorowa Street; the main shopping street. Emma had been to apartment A there so she knew they were around the back. She parked her Corolla before grabbing her small clutch of essentials. Emma checked herself in the reflection of a tinted car window, fine; she walked slightly awkwardly in her stilettos to see apartments A, B and C were on the ground floor. With sweaty hands and her heart racing, Emma knocked on the door, to be greeted by a big guy in a motorcycle t-shirt, jeans, tattoos, a can of beer and a subdued smile.

"Hi, I'm Lucy," Emma said.

He smiled brighter. "I'm Trev; come in."

Emma entered the apartment living room nicer than her living room, especially the leather lounge suite, but it also had varnished pine table and chairs and a laminate kitchen. Standing around were three big guys a bit like Trev: 30s, bikie types.

"These are Mick, Dave and Mason."

Hands were shook while Emma hoped they didn't notice she was still shaking.

"Drink?"

They all had tins of beer but Emma didn't drink when working. "Just water will be fine."

Trev went to the kitchen where moments later Emma had a glass of not quite cold water which she sipped.

"Are you passing through Young?" she asked.

"Yeah, we are," Mason said.

"I didn't see any motorcycles."

"Sydney to Young is a long ride on a motorcycle."

"I expect it would be."

"Now, money," Trev said. "One thousand, eight-hundred for the lot for two hours."

Emma nodded her head while Trev gave her a bundle of 100 dollar bills. Emma quickly flicked through the bundle while thinking these were drug-dealing bikies who knew Josh because of that. *What a small world?* She counted 18 and put them in her clutch.

This way," Trev said as he stood at a doorway.

Emma passed Trev into a bedroom with a king-sized bed, while feeling tiny surrounded by this big guys. Trev took her in her arms to kiss her while a pair of thick, bikie fingers successfully worked the knot on her bikini top before unzipping her miniskirt which fell, revealing her g-string while Emma stepped out of leather bunched at her ankles. Those thick fingers massaged her bottom as Trev massaged her breasts while kissing, and someone's fingers were between her legs, then behind her g-string. And there was another not currently engaged, probably watching. Emma's heart raced and raced, and she was so wet she knew she wouldn't need lube, except for anal.

"Ever done a double penetration before?" Trev whispered in her ear.

"No, but I'm sure it'll be good."

"It will be memorable."

Emma glanced out the corner of her eye at the fourth bikie, Mike, watching while seated on the big bed. She eased away from the others to straddle Mike's knees and kiss him while someone's fingers were inside her g-string again, and another pair of hands massaged her bottom again. Emma knew this was going to be good.

## Chapter Seventeen

Emma woke sore, quite sore, but the soreness of incredible, uninhibited, even unforgettable pleasure. Many guys tried to get her off, some did but most didn't, so she finished herself when they were gone, but not yesterday. Instead she had so many orgasms she began to feel dizzy and had to tell them to stop for a moment, which like everything else in those few hours, they did good naturedly.

Emma rolled onto her back. Somehow her once a month treat escalated into once a day or sometimes even more. Boredom: her job had been a few hours a day, three days a week, sweeping and cleaning at a hairdressing salon. Somehow she got sucked into ice, and to pay for her habit she took one of the few things that paid well. Surprisingly she didn't mind that side of her life: the guys were mostly nice, some were lovely even. Mostly married guys not getting it at home, travellers passing through, again often married and not getting it, and sometimes younger guys without girlfriends, like James which was initially embarrassing, but after money was exchanged became friendly. Even though Emma didn't have any feelings for James, or not enough to date him; that became like a paid date. James was now a regular for his one-hour paid dates.

If Emma could cut back on her ice, no, stop with ice altogether, and keep the rest of her life as it was. She had her own home with independence from her unhappy parents, money to support herself; but she didn't want to be craving. Emma sighed. She had to get clean, now. Emma got up, walked to the bathroom but walked slowly, and after showering she dressed in jeans and a t-shirt, a look she knew suited her, before a mug of coffee and heading out on a cloudy but warm day.

Emma hated hospitals, hated just parking in the hospital grounds, but the Alcohol and Drug Service was in the grounds of the Young District Hospital. It was a house-like building with a tall, red-tiled roof. Inside a 20-something receptionist in a light blue uniform stared at a computer terminal before turning to face Emma.

"Can I help you?" was the not unexpected question.

"I'm here to get help," Emma said.

"Fill out one of these," as a clipboard with a pen was handed across. Emma sat on a vinyl chair to fill out the form: name, date of birth, occupation which she left blank, next of kin so her parents; then more specific details. When finished, Emma signed it and handed it back. The receptionist scanned the form.

"The nurse will be with you in a moment."

"Thank you."

Emma waited for not so long. A middle-aged nurse in the same light blue uniform, came to the door.

"Emma Edwards?" the nurse called.

Emma got up to follow the nurse deeper into that small house, to an office with a desk strewn with papers everywhere, two filing cabinets and an examination bed. The nurse with a name tag Alice sat in her chair while indicating for Emma to sit opposite.

"I'm Alice," in case Emma couldn't read.

"I'm Emma," she said, even though the clipboard and form was on top of the mess on Alice's desk.

"You want to get clean from methamphetamine?"

"I do, as soon as possible."

"Any health problems, STIs; anything like that?"

"I just want to stop these cravings."

"For our part we'll help you as much as we can, while this will take a lot of effort on your part. We offer a number of programs where the most appropriate for you would be counselling, which is available in Cowra."

Cowra wasn't far. "I'm interested," Emma said.

"I can give you a health check now, if you want."

"I've only been using heavily for a few months."

"That's good; that gives you a good chance for recovery. Let me see when I can get you an appointment."

Nurse Alice turned to a computer screen to type briefly then frown. "Is Friday the 17th of April at four in the afternoon good for you?"

So long! "Isn't there anything sooner?"

"I'm afraid not. Should I book you in?"

141

"Yes please," Emma said.

Soon Emma was on her way with an appointment card in her hand, feeling terribly, terribly down. Burdened. She woke with a clear goal: get clean and leave the rest as it was, and now this delay. More than three months to wait before she could even start – then Emma had an idea. They might be able to help. Emma headed to her car.

* * *

Headspace Young was quiet that Friday morning, which was a good sign for Young: no youth crises demanding her attention, but bad for Chloe. A day dragged when there was nothing to do. Then someone came through the door; Chloe looked up to see a young woman, hard to pick her age but perhaps early twenties. Tall, full-figured but in good shape, long brown hair in a ponytail, dressed simply in jeans and a white t-shirt.

"Hi, I'm Chloe.

"Hi, I'm Emma.

"Welcome to Headspace. Take a seat," Chloe said as she moved to the couch. "Do you want a drink?"

"Water will be fine."

Chloe took two glasses to fill from the water cooler. She gave one to Emma who smiled.

"Environmentally friendly," Emma said.

Not a disposable plastic cup; young Millennials were switched-on that way. Chloe sat beside Emma with her glass.

"What can I do for you, Emma?"

"No forms to fill out?"

"Only if you want to!"

"No, no, no!  Alright, I'll start.  I'm Emma as I said and I'm 19, and I have a problem with meth that I would like to deal with."

"How big a problem?"

"I started once a month, then once a fortnight, then once a week and now it's once a day.  Now I need it – you know."

"How long have you been using?"

"Once a day these past few months."

"Are you working?"

"Not really."

"How do you pay?"

A pause while Emma contemplated her glass.  "I'm an escort," she said before looking to Chloe.

"Is that a problem?" Chloe asked.

"No.  I was using and I needed money, so now I'm an escort."

"I understand," Chloe said.  Drugs – escort rather than escort – drugs because of self-loathing.

"There's no other way to make a living," Emma said, "unlike our parents who could leave school and get jobs, and keep their jobs for years.  These days you need a university degree."

"Not even then," Chloe said. "Many university graduates put in all that effort and incur big debts to get their degrees, only to take whatever they can find. Maybe even escorting. These days to be guaranteed a career you need a masters or a doctorate."

"Really? No, you have this job here."

"Many but not all graduates. In a way I was lucky."

"I made it through year 12 but only just, so not a degree and definitely not a masters! School just isn't my thing. Regardless of that, I just want to get clean from ice."

"Of course." Chloe reached to her desk to grab the folded pamphlet to hand to Emma. "Read this and tell me what you think."

Chloe watch Emma frown, turn the page, frown deeper, turn more and then hold it while looking to the floor.

"I need to deal with cravings, difficulty sleeping, agitation and irritability, aches and pains, and mood swings, and I need a safe place, support, and a plan for afterwards. "Does this work?" she asked while looking up.

"It can. Do you have a safe place?"

"I rent my own unit."

"A support person? I can help you as much as I can, but you need someone there for you anytime, day or night."

Emma frowned. "I think I have a support person: my ex-boyfriend and his girlfriend. His new girlfriend."

"Would he?" Chloe asked; surprised.

144

"We both realise what he has now isn't what we had then, so now we're friends."

"And his girlfriend?"

"She's lovely."

"Your plan for afterwards?"

"As I am now: my own home and escorting." Emma looked into Chloe's eyes. "I earn good money and I meet nice people, and it's alright."

"Do you use protection?"

Silence for a moment. "Yeah I do."

Chloe knew that wasn't the case, or not always the case. Guys often pestered girls and often offered more. Chloe wondered how to frame that.

"Condoms don't protect from all STIs so you should get yourself tested every three months," she said. "Cowra Health Service is discreet and offers free testing. I'll give you their card."

Chloe went to her desk to get a card from the many cards in her top drawer, and another card. She sat on the couch to give the card to Emma, and the other card.

"You have my card, so if you need help beyond what your support person can do for you, ring me. If I can help I will, or come here anytime we're open."

"Thanks Chloe."

"And remember, three month testing!"

"I will I promise."

145

"If you have any other problems, don't hesitate because we're here to help young people like you."

"Young people have it tough these days," Emma said with her natural effervescence dissipated. "Something's gone wrong when you need a masters or to be a doctor to get a proper job."

Chloe drew a deep breath. "You're right, Emma. If I could change things, I would."

"I know you would."

Emma stood straight and tall while holding the pamphlet. Chloe stood too.

"With your pamphlet and help from my friends, I'm certain I'll be good."

"Your attitude is your most important asset in this, Emma. With your attitude I'm certain you will be good."

"Thank you so much, Chloe. Soon I'll be seeing you to tell you I'm clean."

"I'll be looking forward to that."

She left while Chloe hoped that Emma would really be good. The rest of Chloe's day was quiet apart from a visit from Matthew Wall, Matt, who's only hope was professional rehab given he lived with a drug-addicted girlfriend who had alcoholic parents. Even after rehab, unlike Emma, Matt didn't stand a chance. He would fall into old habits for sure.

Chloe was still thinking about her day later that evening.

"You're far away," Luke said.

"Sorry, Chloe apologised. "I had a new girl, addicted to meth and working as an escort to pay for her habit. She wants to get clean which I think she has a chance to, and she wants to continue as an escort because that's the only way for her to make a living."

"Is it?" Luke asked.

"In a way it is. Escorting has its own set of challenges which we didn't discuss. Sexual health is one but relationships are a problem too. Another thing is the money. They can give it up, perhaps because they find a boyfriend, but the money often lures them back."

"Almost addictive."

"Not really," Emma said. "It's more that regular work these days, unless you have a special skill like you or me, is scarce. Too scarce."

"Not everyone can train to be a police officer because there aren't enough positions; or a counsellor either. Something has gone wrong." Luke frowned. "That's why we have the need for Headspace for young people, and counsellors like you."

"We need to think beyond plugging leaking dykes."

"Socialism?" Luke asked.

"Capitalism in its present form isn't working."

Luke looked thoughtful, while the more Chloe spent with good young people like Emma, the more she was sure they needed to radical overhaul Australian society, which surely

147

would come as an older and more settled generation was replaced by the young and the unsettled. Chloe hoped that necessary changes, whatever form they took, would in time rescue this generation from the hopelessness that many faced.

## Chapter Eighteen

After a couple of cloudy days almost threatening much-needed rain given the east coast of Australia was on fire, Saturday dawned fine and sunny. With 18 million hectares burned so far, more than 2,700 houses destroyed, 34 lives lost, and ash falling as far away as New Zealand, never-ending fine weather was terribly disappointing. The worst drought ever had caused the worst bushfires ever. An older generation acknowledged climate change, promised action on climate change yet did nothing, leaving Josh and his generation an uninhabitable planet.

With poached eggs, coffee and toast for breakfast, Josh felt a totally down even though they had two days together.

"You look upset," Sophie said; which was observant.

"Yeah."

"It is what it is and not here. Get your mind off it. Let's go swimming."

"I'm sure they're not prepared for swimming."

"You know they don't need to be!"

It had been a while since their last time. "You can ask them."

For some reason Josh and Sophie were always last to arrive, to sit amongst the group under the same tree each Saturday. They all looked fine; unlike Josh the tragedy playing out some hundreds of kilometres to the east didn't register. Emma really glowed.

"Seeing as it's hot today, do you want to go swimming?" Sophie said. "Before you say anything, rule is no bathers or bikinis."

"Yeah, let's go swimming," James said.

"Let's," Emma said.

Sophie stood. "Let's go now!" she announced.

With Sophie leading they went to their cars, to end up at Koorawatha Falls not so far away. If such a thing was possible it was even dryer and even dustier, but once stripped off and in cold but muddy water, laughing and playing, Josh forgot his troubles.

"Josh!" Sophie called out.

Josh turned to have Sophie jump at him, for him to catch her with her arms around his shoulders and her legs around his waist, kissing him.

Suddenly they got drenched. Josh let Sophie go to fall backwards into the water, to turn and see Emma laughing brightly. He splashed her as big as he could and soon they had a huge water fight. Two against one had a predictable outcome.

"Alright, you win!" Emma admitted with her hands in the air.

Josh was relieved by Emma's good humour towards him; Trev and his mates must have treated her well. Later they returned to the sparsely grassed bank. Sophie lay stomach-down; Josh lay beside and Emma lay beside Josh.

"I have a favour to ask," Emma said. "I want to get clean but I need help."

"Of course I'll help you," Josh said without hesitation.

"Me too," Sophie said.

"I have a pamphlet I can show you later, but it's just a list of things I'll go through, that I'll need a support person which will be you two, and for me to think about my plans for the future. Before you ask, I'll keep doing what I'm doing now."

"You like it," Josh said as a statement.

"It's fine."

"What does a support person do?" Josh asked.

"It's not really specific. Maybe call in and maybe I can ring you if I'm in trouble."

Josh thought. "I'll call by every morning, to start."

"Thanks."

"When do you start?" Sophie asked.

"Today. It takes a few days before it hits me."

"Good luck and I'll call by – each afternoon."

"Thank you Sophie."

"I know everything," Sophie obliquely. "After, anytime, you can talk with me. You're my best friend."

Josh's stomach grumbled while Emma chuckled.

"Let's eat lunch," she said.

Emma sat with Josh and Sophie to share scrambled egg sandwiches and cordial, of course.

"My mother says two things," Sophie said. "Well she says more than two things, but the two most important things are: we're not all poured from the same mould, and don't do anything that harms you or anyone else." Sophie looked to Emma sitting across. "This is the reason why we're naked here. In any case, do guys ever want to do drugs with you?"

"No," Emma said, "and if they did I'd give their money back and tell them to go."

"Are you ever worried about your safety?"

"Sometimes, but wives are at more risk – aren't they?"

"That's true. Any nice guys?"

"They're mostly nice."

"Nice enough to go further?"

"Many are married."

"If they're married and – you know; then I think they're fair game."

"I suppose so but there's an age difference."

"My mother's partner is 15 years older than her, and she's so much in love with him."

"And he loves her," Josh said while surprised by the 15 years. Jack showed his age well.

"I hadn't thought of that," Emma said. "I'll keep an open mind. If I meet someone, I'll stop."

"Could you study now, in case you stop in the future?" Sophie asked.

"I'm not a university person," Emma said firmly.

"TAFE teaches us practical skills to help us get decent jobs, and isn't as hard as university. My cousin told me TAFE is than better than school for her because it's practical, where with school she struggled to see the relevance."

"Your cousin finds it easier because they're teaching her things she wants to learn," Emma said. "I see the sense in that. I could do a TAFE certificate, I suppose, and that way I could get a decent job, if there is such a thing."

"Well, you have the TAFE here or there's distance learning."

Emma sat up and crossed her legs with her eyes sparkling. "This is a great idea, Sophie. Study will fill in my time on – quiet days. Because my hours aren't set I'll do distance learning." Emma sipped her cordial. "I had to get out of my parent's house," she then said. "Maybe they once loved each other but now it's so strained. It was horrible to be there. Now that I've seen you two together I realise my brother and his wife aren't in love, either."

Silence.

"This is why marriages fail," Emma said.

"Right," Josh said.

"I'm glad I know this now."

Josh looked over Koorawatha which was more than a small lake surrounded by gum trees in the midst of parched fields. There were wattle trees too, thick and green, magpies warbling, tiny green lorikeets feeding close by, several grey kangaroos looking on curiously, a light breeze blowing, giving relief from summer's heat while sitting in the dappled shade of tall gum trees. Then kookaburras called which sent a shiver up Josh's spine.

Glen came to sit beside Emma.

"You've got your own little group within a group," he said.

"Glen," Josh said, "In Sydney do they have lakes like this surrounded by trees, with magpies, lorikeets, kookaburras and kangaroos?"

Glen laughed. "In Sydney they hardly have trees! They call themselves Australians but Sydney isn't Australia. Australia is anywhere north, south or west. Especially here in the west."

"You're glad to be home," Emma said.

"It's great to be back in Young, naked here with my friends. Getting by on money too. Mum and Kev are on disability pensions so I get full Youth Allowance. That's decent money."

"How is it at home?" Emma asked. She knew, of course.

"Too much smoking and drinking, the odd argument, but not enough to force me out the door."

"Do you have a girlfriend?" Sophie asked.

"You have a one-track mind, Sophie! I've been looking but I've not found anyone new."

"How about someone younger?"

"Hannah's friends – no, your friends.  Yeah," Glen said; nodding his head.

"So you're interested?"

"Are any of your friends looking for a boyfriend?"

"All girls are looking even when they're not looking."

"All boys look when they're not looking, you know," and he laughed.

"School's busy with assignments already, but a Saturday night date is possible."

"Like there's time for you to have a Saturday afternoon swim."

"Like swimming today and the party tonight.  Lucy is nice, grown-up and smart, and pretty.  I can ask Lucy if she wants a date with the twin brother of my boyfriend."

"Non-identical, younger twin brother."

"I thought twins were the same ages?" Sophie asked with brow furrowed.

"Josh is a few minutes older."

"Ha!  I'll ask Lucy, and if she's interested I'll text you her number."

"A Saturday night date," Glen said.  "What do you think, Sophie?"

"Take Lucy to the Mandarin Court; it's great there.  If your date goes well make sure you have a date for Sunday.  You could take Lucy to the Chinese Gardens."

"Yeah, you're right. That would make a good pair of dates. Thanks Sophie."

Emma stood. "Another swim?" she shouted to all.

They all stood, to race to the water on a hot summer's day with the coastal strip of the state of New South Wales, and of other states of Australia, burning to the ground.

## Chapter Nineteen

Josh finished his bowl of Nutri Grain then drained the last of his coffee. Oddly, on weekdays he missed eggs and toast.

"How's your friend?" Jack asked.

"Yesterday she was a bit down," Josh said. "I'm sure it's going to get worse for her before it gets better."

"That's true."

"I'm going to see her now." Josh stood. "Need anything while I'm out?"

"Can you get two litres of milk?" Jessica asked.

"No problems Jessica."

"Thanks."

Josh headed out for the short drive to Emma's unit where he parked in the shade of a gum tree before pressing the buzzer. Emma opened it, untidy and unkempt. She held the door open while Josh stepped inside to near darkness.

"I need a hit," she murmured.

"You know we spoke about that," Josh said.

"Yeah, I know. Can you hug me instead?"

Josh didn't want to hug Emma, even though they were just friends these days. Instead he held her hand and then both hands.

"That's nice," Emma murmured.

"I do like you, Emma, and I hope we'll always be friends."

"Me too."

"Is there anything I can do?"

"Coffee would be good."

Josh filled her kettle, switched it on to spoon Bushels and sugar into two mugs. He took a milk plastic bottle, sniffed it and it wasn't off but made a mental note to buy fresh milk for Emma in a few days time, and anything else she needed. Soon they had mugs of coffee in her living room.

"Last night I didn't sleep much," Emma said.

That was in the pamphlet from Headspace. "Do you want me to get something from the chemist? The pamphlet recommended that."

"If you can. I don't want to see a doctor for a prescription. I don't think I'm up for explaining all of this again," and Emma sort-of smiled.

"I'm sure they'll have something. I know from Hannah that anti-histamines make you drowsy, so a couple of those should work."

"Really?"

Josh nodded his head. "Hannah used to sleep for hours! Couldn't get her out of bed next morning!"

"You're a really useful support person." Emma put her empty mug down. "We both got out of dysfunctional homes, didn't we?"

They certainly did. "One day, Mum and Kev will have one or the other in hospital, or worse, while your parents were opposites of that. It was chilling to see them resent each other's presence so much. I can't understand why they stayed together."

"Money I think. They'd bought and paid for the house, raised two children, and somewhere on that journey they'd fallen out of love, but they'd paid off their house and only had to pay their bills."

"You're better away from that darkness," Josh said.

"I can work from here too. I've told clients who've rung I'm sick for two weeks."

"So they'll ring back?"

"Yeah."

"The pamphlet said 7 to 28 days, so maybe two weeks for you."

"I'm hoping that's as long as this takes. I have a home, I'm making good money, and I will do distance learning so I'll have something for later. Maybe one day I'll find a boyfriend. Maybe even an older boyfriend."

"That's the mould thing Sophie was talking about. The partner for Jessica is different to other women, but don't rule out even 15 years. What would that be?"

"That would be 34. Those things Sophie said about everyone being different, which we tend to forget, like university isn't for me, and also no harm, were really astute. She must have the best mother of us all."

"Yeah Jessica's great!" Josh exclaimed.

"She might be your mother-in-law one day."

159

"And you might be Sophie's bridesmaid."

"Ha!  Actually, seeing as you're living together, you'll be legally married in time."

Josh rubbed his chin.  "I'm not sure how long that is."

"For Centrelink it's the moment you live together while the rest is two years."

"Ah; a long time."

"Promise me you won't lose Sophie in the meantime.  I want to see you two, together forever."

"Me too."  Josh saw a change in Emma, from really down to a brighter now.  "Do you feel better?"

"After coffee and friendly chat – yes I do very much.  Thank you."

"I'll pick Sophie up after school and we'll see you then.  At the same time I'll bring something to help you sleep."

"Thanks Josh, you're the best."

"No you're the best, Emma, for making this effort.  Never forget that."

"Thank you, yes."

"What now for the rest your day?" Josh asked.

"I might look at distance learning courses."

"Enjoy.  See you Emma."

"See you Josh."

Josh left feeling bright with a spring in his step, and remembered he had to buy milk on the way home, too.

* * *

The younger children, really they were children, always raced out the gate, boys their age raced too; really they were children too. The older girls walked slowly behind.

"My boyfriend has a non-identical twin brother, Glen," Sophie said to Lucy. "He's nice and he's free. Would you be interested in meeting him one Saturday night, for dinner at a restaurant?"

Lucy frowned. "Is he nice?"

"I've met Glen a few times and he's totally nice."

"What about our assignments?"

"Like Josh year 12 is recent for Glen, so like Josh your school work will take priority, but that doesn't mean you can't see each other on weekends, when you have time."

"Alright."

"If you give me your number I can text him."

"My number is...."

"Hang on," Sophie said as she got her Galaxy out.

"My number is 0452 189 111."

Sophie typed that into an empty message, to text to Glen later.

"Now I'm nervous!" Lucy exclaimed.

"It's just a date. If you like each other there'll be more dates. There's Josh now."

"Does Glen have a car?"

"He's older so he has a car. See you Lucy."

"See you Sophie."

Sophie ran to Josh to kiss him while hoping everyone would see her do that! Then she threw her backpack on the backseat before climbing in front for Josh to drive to Emma's unit where he parked in the shade of a tree. Sophie followed Josh to the front door where he pressed the buzzer. The door opened to reveal Emma looking pale and drawn. They entered Emma's darkened unit where Josh gave Emma a small packet.

"Take two of these a few hours before you want to sleep," Josh said. "It won't be as good as a natural sleep and you might wake up still feeling tired, but it will be better than little or no sleep."

"Thanks Josh."

"How are you?" Sophie asked.

"You've used, haven't you?" Emma asked.

"I've used a bit but not more than once a fortnight."

"I really want a total high, you know, but I won't. I want my highs in life to be natural, not tied to ice and a bong. So even though I want it I won't." Emma looked up to catch Josh's eyes. "That pamphlet is really good, especially about anger! I was looking at distance learning on the internet but it was running so slow. I totally lost it and instead of smashing my computer I punched the wall instead! Fuck that hurt! I feel like – an awful person for doing that."

"That's the drugs, not you," Josh said. "In time that will go. Did you find any courses?"

162

"I thought counselling but then I thought there are only a few counselling jobs inland and I don't want to move to Sydney. I've been there a few times and I hate Sydney. Then I looked for jobs in inland New South Wales, but the internet was running slow so I punched the wall and that was enough for today. I'll look tomorrow."

Sophie knew one option. "Health and medical is everywhere," she said.

"I don't want to work in aged care."

"Medical receptionist or something like that?"

"Yeah," Emma said slowly. "Every doctor's surgery."

"Pathology, radiology."

"Drug and alcohol centres," and Emma laughed. "I'll look for that later. What do you want to do?"

"I want to do hairdressing."

"That's everywhere too."

"Yes it is."

"You're a country girl like me.

Sophie nodded her head.

"Are you good for something to eat?" Sophie asked.

"I'm not really hungry but I need to keep my energy up. Something simple like baked beans on toast, easy to digest when you're not craving food, and then a good night's sleep."

Sophie sensed Emma's desperation so she stood. "Come here," Sophie said; which Emma did for Sophie to hug her.

163

Hugged and hugged. Eventually they moved apart with Emma's eyes glistening.

"I'll see you tomorrow," Sophie said, not wanting to leave but she had too much school work.

"Thanks."

They left. Outside, Sophie followed Josh to his car parked in the shade. Soon they were heading home with Sophie contemplating her next assignment.

# Chapter Twenty

Although they were the same age and grew up together, Josh was always more advanced. That was why Glen went to Sydney: to prove he could live in the city and to get away from being shaded. After a while it was ridiculous to be in Sydney when home was better, so now Glen had a date courtesy of Josh's second girlfriend. Josh's first girlfriend Emma was the reason Glen left for Sydney; Mum hated Emma staying in Josh's room while Glen felt uncomfortable – no jealous. Momentarily Glen wondered why he didn't ask Emma, or other girls their age, until he realised he was terrified of being rejected. Then Glen knew why he was comfortable calling Lucy; thanks to Josh she was expecting Glen to invite her out and she wouldn't reject him. Glen keyed her number.

"Hi," she answered.

"Hi Lucy, I'm Glen."

"Hi Glen, I've been expecting you! How are you?"

"I'm fine; how are you?"

"Great. What are you doing?"

"Apart from ringing to ask you to go out tomorrow night? I'm studying for a Certificate Four in Business Administration."

"Ah, that's good. You know I'm doing year 12."

"I know you are and I know that can be busy, but I hope you can go out with tomorrow night?"

165

"I need to get away from schoolwork!" she exclaimed.

"Is it alright to pick you up at seven?"

"Seven's good, I'll text you my address. I'm looking forward to this."

"Me too."

"See you."

"Bye."

Moments later after 'ting' for a message, Glen had Lucy's address. Too easy!

* * *

Glen pressed the buzzer beside the front door of a brick veneer house in the quiet suburbs of Young, a lot like the house his mother rented. But if Lucy's parents hadn't divorced like his parents, they might own that house. The door opened to reveal Lucy with a bright smile, squeezed into a sleeveless black dress that couldn't possibly have been lower, shorter, or tighter. Bare legs, black stiletto heels, silver locket, silver bracelet and a black clutch. Lucy reminded Glen of Emma being thicker, while totally beautiful with fair skin, deep blue eyes, long jet black hair half-way down her back, and her smile framed in luscious red lipstick. That was a lovely look. With a fair complexion and big eyes, she didn't need more than lipstick.

"Hi Lucy, I'm Glen."

"Hi Glen."

"Let's go."

Glen walked with Lucy, a little unsteady on her heels, to his car where she climbed in for the short drive to the Mandarin Court Chinese restaurant in Boorowa Street. Glen was able to park quite close, while inside the waiter at the rostrum checked Glen's booking before showing them to a table for two and unfolding starched napkins. They didn't stay like that for long: Lucy brought her chair to beside Glen to sit side-by-side for selfies for Instagram. After that she looked even happier.

"This is my first date!" she exclaimed.

Glen found Lucy's bright smile infectious as the waiter came to order drinks. Glen ordered two glasses of white wine while knowing Lucy wasn't old enough. She was pleased with his choice of drink, though. Pleased with everything: Glen's idea to order a couple of dishes to share, to try chopsticks which he showed her how to use, another glass of wine each, and everything to do with her first date.

"Sophie said you're a younger twin," Lucy asked. "How can that be?"

"I won't go into too many details, but imagine one then two. I'm a couple of minutes younger."

"Ah. Sophie has a boyfriend and she's doing well with her schoolwork and she said I can do the same. There's always some free time, isn't there?"

"We're both studying but if we're careful, I think this can work."

"Yeah, be careful in all things!" and Lucy laughed. Glen suspected innuendo there but probably for a later date. Although with Lucy in her tiny dress he wouldn't have needed much persuasion.

After honey king prawns, Mongolian beef and fried rice, followed by fried ice cream each for dessert: good food and great service, not to mention two glasses of wine for an underage drinker, it had been a great night when Glen drove Lucy home. There in that quiet, suburban street Glen touched Lucy's bare arm, her other arm, drew her closer to kiss her cheek, and briefly kiss her lips, warm on a cool summer's evening, and still while holding her, her eyes closed in the light from a nearby streetlight, he kissed her longer and just nudged her lips with his tongue. Glen's first kiss.

"Do you want another date?" Glen asked.

"Yes," she almost whispered. "Yes I do."

"I can pick you up tomorrow. Is ten good?"

"Ten is good."

Glen couldn't help himself, he kissed her again.

"Goodnight Lucy."

"Goodnight Glen.

He watched her, especially her hips in that tight dress, as she walked to her front door to disappear out of sight.

* * *

Glen heard his phone 'ting' with a message. He picked it up to see a message from Lucy with a picture attachment. 'thnx for the evening had a gr8 time sent a present'.

Glen pressed the image for it to download and open. Amazing! Lucy in red lingerie: a red lace bra, matching red lace panties and red stockings. Beautiful and she had a cute figure, not totally slim like girls in the internet but really – cute, especially framed like that.

Ting for another message. 'ive shown you mine now you show me yours'.

Glen pondered, then thought: *why not?* He took off his shoes, socks, shirt and trousers, pressed the camera app, put his phone at full arm's length, and took his picture in grey boxer briefs. He checked his picture while thinking men didn't have anything like the same appeal in underwear, but he was slim and defined. Glen composed a text: 'yours is gr8 this is mine'; attached his picture and sent it.

Shortly after another 'ting' with an attachment. 'yours is gr8 too this is more'.

Now sweaty and with his heart racing, Glen opened the attachment. It was what he expected, Lucy without lingerie. Simply beautiful especially her breasts, but really all of her: totally beautiful. Totally incredible!

Ting. 'i've shown you mine now you show me yours'.

Glen was expecting that next. He took off his briefs, and after Lucy's latest picture he was fully hard too. He took a

169

selfie then composed a message. 'your totally beautiful this is mine'. He sent it.

A few moments later. 'your totally handsome wait five minutes'.

Glen waited while wondering. No – he knew! Sometime later, 'ting'. Glen opened the message: 'this is me hot'. Glen opened a video attachment: Lucy had her phone resting near floor level: still naked, cupping one breast while she rubbed between her legs, smooth and hairless. Rubbed and rubbed with two fingers, eyes closed. Rubbed and rubbed and rubbed, before taking her hand from between her legs and blowing him a kiss. Incredible: so much better than porn on the internet, while Lucy wasn't thick but simply the most beautiful woman Glen had ever seen. The style of girls in porn didn't reflect the full range of feminine beauty.

Ting. 'i've shown you mine now you show me yours'.

Glen expected that too. He composed: 'five minutes' and sent his message.

Ting. 'kk'.

Glen switched his camera to video, then put his phone down and pressed 'record'. Now with his eyes closed he stroked lightly while thinking he might be a turn-on for Lucy. He imagined her watching him, perhaps rubbing herself to come, and that was totally hot. Glen stroked lightly like that for a time, and then gave a two thumbs-up with a big smile. He picked up his phone to turn the camera off, composed a message: 'yours was gr8 this is mine'. Glen attached his clip and sent it.

Some minutes later. 'nice but you didn't come'.

'did you'.

'wait a moment'.

Glen waited for quite a while until 'ting'. 'seeing you like that made me hotter'.

The next clip showed Lucy on her back on her bed, phone standing between her legs, as she rubbed with her camera really close. Rubbed and rubbed and rubbed.

Ting. 'I came for you'.

Glen had no choice. He knelt on his bed with his phone almost under, and after reaching for his tube of KY lube he stroked himself properly this time. Stroked and stroked and stroked until he felt it tingle, then more than tingle, then until he came.

Glen wiped greasy fingers on his discarded underwear, switched the camera off, opened a blank text and sent it.

About five minutes later: 'nice now I sleep naked sweet dreams'.

Glen composed: 'now I sleep naked too sweet dreams'. Send.

After all of that, and especially after coming for Lucy, Glen was sure he would sleep well with sweet dreams.

\* \* \*

Glen sat on soft grass shaded by gum trees. Lucy snuggled up against him, his arm around her. Touts Lookout just off the highway north of Young, was serene and had a beautiful view across the dry, yellow plains of farms around Young, towards blue-tinged hills in the far distance. Later they would drive to Cowra further north, perhaps for lunch at the cafe at the Japanese Gardens, but for now Glen knew that peaceful beauty was all they needed.

## Chapter Twenty One

Sophie lay in bed with rain loudly beating against the corrugated iron roof. So heavy, amazing! She felt great. For sure this rain would put those fires out, give farmers a chance to recover; give Young a chance to recover, the state, the country even.

"Let's fuck," Josh said about the noise.

"Fuck yeah!"

*What a great way to celebrate!*

Sophie now slept naked like Josh, so simply rolled onto her side to hug him with his hardness pressed against her stomach, and her wetness mirroring wetness outside as rain hammered against their roof. Josh rolled onto his back while Sophie rolled on top. Kneeling now, his hands on her bottom, she fed him inside her.

* * *

Sophie switched on the kettle, went to the cupboard for the packet of cereal, took a bowl from the lower cupboard, and poured herself her usual, weekday breakfast. In that kitchen it was cosy with rain beating against the window. She leaned against the counter to eat as Josh came into the room. He took a bowl, the packet Sophie left out, then when the kettle switched off, Josh made two mugs of coffee. He put one beside Sophie who sipped it. Nice.

"Do you want a lift to school?" he asked.

Sophie expected that. "Yes please."

Josh ate and drank as Sophie finished her bowl. She went to the bathroom to brush her teeth; then she grabbed the blue raincoat she previously used at Wagga Wagga High School on wet days, and her backpack. After last night's heavy downpour, rain was steady now. Sophie slung her backpack onto the back seat to climb in and buckle-up. Josh was ready to go.

"When I was young a wet day was a bad day but now I see things differently," Sophie said.

"I'm the same." Josh started up to pull out. "It'll take more than a night and a day of rain after this long drought," he then said.

"This is a start – no, this gives us hope."

Josh nodded his head as he turned onto the Olympic Way, drove through the centre of town, and further south where he parked amongst more cars than normal. Sophie had a bit of a walk from there but she was prepared with her raincoat. She kissed Josh's cheek.

"See you Josh."

"See you Sophie."

With her backpack slung over her coat, Sophie followed many students inside to the year 12 lockers. There was Lucy showing her smartphone to a group of their friends: Kayla, Alana, Amy and Ann, all talking excitedly. Sophie went to them.

"What is it?" she asked.

Lucy snatched her phone away while blushing bright red. "Nothing."

That was something but if Lucy didn't want to show, she didn't want to show. There was something else.

"How did your date with Glen go?" Sophie asked.

"Oh our date was great!" Lucy exclaimed while Ann giggled. "We went out all day Sunday as well."

"And other things," Kayla said.

Sophie raised her eyebrows. "We hugged and kissed a bit," Lucy said. "I like Glen; thank you for arranging this. Twin brothers now dating two girls in year 12."

The bell rang. Sophie stowed her raincoat and backpack before grabbing textbooks, notebooks and her pencil case for her first two subjects. She was glad Lucy's date went well, especially for Glen. Glen was nice, not like Josh who was nice while having an interesting side to his nature, but she knew Glen would treat Lucy well, even if not as interesting as his brother. Sophie followed those girls still in a tight group; talking amongst themselves in hushed voices.

* * *

Kev did nothing useful around the house while the garden became ever-messier. Soon Glen would have to cut grass, prune shrubs and probably poison weeds. And rake scoria that birds threw onto now muddy grass when they were digging for worms. Glen went to the garage to check on the pruning sheers which were hanging on a hook, the sprayer

175

and to see if there was enough glyphosate in the bottle, which there was, and the lawn rake, except the lawn rake had several broken tines. Oh well, they weren't expensive and he wanted to see Josh anyway.

Back in his car on a day of much-needed steady rain, to drive to Boorowa Street and Mitre 10. In the gardening department, Josh looked somewhat bored.

"Hi Josh."

"Hi Glen."

"I'm after a rake to clear scoria from grass."

Josh reached to rakes in a bin to pull one out. "This one will do the job; it's 15 99. How did it go with Sophie's friend?"

"Lucy and I had a great time. Thank Sophie for me." Glen wondered but he sort-of wanted to show off. "Lucy sent me some pictures."

Glen took his iPhone from his pocket, opened his downloaded images and gave it to Josh who frowned while he swiped.

"She's gorgeous, she reminds me of Emma which is a compliment, but prettier. Definitely a pretty girl." Josh moved close to hand the phone back. "Be careful who you show those to, or better, don't show anyone," he whispered. "You could be convicted for having child pornography while Lucy could be convicted for making child pornography."

Glen hadn't thought of that but Josh was right. "I'll show you and that's all." Then he thought more. "That's a ridiculous law."

"Not only that but you or she or both of you will become registered sex offenders, which will stain you for the rest of your lives."

Glen hadn't thought of that either. "That's even more ridiculous. I mean there's nothing we can't do consensually together, except take pictures!"

"You don't have to convince me these are ridiculous laws, but this is serious. But beyond that, Lucy is totally gorgeous!"

"We went out on Saturday night and all day Sunday, and I'm seeing her next Saturday."

"Is she your girlfriend yet?"

"She's my girlfriend all but in name. Really, thank Sophie for me."

"I will, but she was also doing a favour for her friend. Sophie said Lucy is grown-up."

"She is."

"There. I'll take you to the register and give you a discount on that rake."

Glen followed Josh to the registers while totally happy he was dating a genuinely attractive girl, but more importantly one of the most friendly and personable, girls in Young. How good was that?

## Chapter Twenty Two

Sophie was glad when the bell rang on a day where it rained for hours but now was just cloudy. She walked with her best friend Lucy, positively glowing; her first date had done her good. Something was odd though: girls and some boys blew kisses at them. One girl pretended to rub herself through her skit which was totally weird.

"Do you know what's up?" Sophie asked Lucy.

"No I don't," Lucy said then stopped. She put her backpack down to rummage through it, and rummage and rummage and rummage. She looked up. "Have you seen my phone?" she asked.

"I haven't seen any phones."

"It's a pink Galaxy with silver stars on the back!" Lucy exclaimed.

"No, I haven't seen that phone."

"Oh no!" Lucy exclaimed before picking her backpack up and running towards the main building. Sophie thought to lose an expensive smartphone was particularly bad; no quite awful. She walked towards the gate.

* * *

In her second week Emma was much better. She said she craved less, she was less angry and her appetite had returned. Emma said her appetite for life had returned. Josh went with Sophie after school for an hour or so, talked with Emma for a while, and then Josh drove Sophie home to finish her

178

assignment from last week. She worked on the dining room table with books spread everywhere while Josh scrolled Instagram on his smartphone. His timeline was particularly busy with a lot happening in Young. Lots of discussion about Lucy and her boyfriend, and actually accusations that Lucy was a slut. Girls were the worst when it came to that. Josh didn't know if that was implications of Lucy being sexual or simply because she dated, although dating didn't deserve being called a slut. More likely jealousy, especially with an older guy. Lucy went on a date and now she was a slut, although Josh was sure all that happened between Glen and Lucy were a few pictures. Those discussions were insistent, though. Josh went deeper and then stopped. Fuck! He recognised Lucy in red lingerie, now public. Then one of the pictures of her naked. Worse: video clips in two carousel posts that Glen hadn't shown. Again Lucy naked: Josh pressed to play – fuck! Everything until she blew a kiss at the end. The second was even more explicit. *Total fuck!*

"What is it?" Sophie asked.

Josh handed his phone to Sophie. "Play those," he said flatly.

Sophie frowned for several minutes, which was as long as they ran in total. "No!" she exclaimed before looking up. "Lucy lost her phone at school today."

That explained it.

179

"I think she showed this to friends and someone might have stolen her phone because of what's on it," Sophie clarified

"She wouldn't have shown those clips to her friends," Josh said while thinking. "Perhaps Glen returned the favour and she showed clips of him."

"You might be right," Sophie said.

"Instagram will delete these and suspend her, but the damage is done. Many have seen this already and some will download them, and her pictures too."

"Pictures?"

"Glen showed me and I told him to keep them secret. They weren't more explicit than those clips, though."

"It's not possible to be more explicit than those clips!" Sophie exclaimed.

That was true unless they filmed themselves together.

"The damage is done," Sophie said. "I fucked up for Glen though."

"It's not your fault," Josh said as he held her hand. "That's Lucy giving Glen a message, I think."

"Yeah, well, it's safer like we did in my room than to spread it all over the internet!"

Too true.

\* \* \*

Once more a daytime shift, Luke fastened his vest before securing his pistol. He entered the Operations Room where Alice was in earnest conversation with Leon.

"Ah, Luke," Leon said. "We have a report of child pornography requiring investigation."

"It's sexting gone wrong," Alice said. "Clearly Young High School isn't aware sexting isn't a crime these days. But this one seems to involve non-consensual posting on social media, which is a crime."

Luke nodded his head in understanding. "Let's go to Young High School, Alice, and see what we can find."

Out back their usual car waited, for Luke to take the wheel for a short drive to the high school, where as was the case with schools during class time, it was eerily quiet. At the office Luke introduced himself and Alice to the receptionist to be shortly after in the office of Principal Paul McCaughan, overlooking an empty, asphalt assembly area. As always Alice had her notebook ready.

"Thank you for coming so quickly," Mr McCaughan started. "Yesterday, some of our teachers were aware something was happening on social media which was engaging many students. We didn't get to the bottom of it until late in the day when cleaners found a smartphone discarded in the women's toilets." Mr McCaughan slid open a drawer to retrieve a ziplock plastic bag containing a pink-coloured smartphone with a couple of silver stars on the back.

"To find who this phone belongs to I went through the contacts. Then I checked other things to discover the source of what was happening on social media. On Facebook I found matching pictures and clips."

Mr McCaughan handed the bag to Luke who guessed what that smartphone contained.

"Are there intimate pictures and clips on this phone?" Luke asked.

"Yes, very intimate. This phone belongs to Lucy Ryan, a normally well-behaved student in year 12."

"Taking, transmitting and possessing intimate pictures of a personal nature isn't a crime these days," Luke clarified, to the obvious surprise of Mr McCaughan. "In this respect your student, Lucy Ryan, hasn't done anything wrong. However stealing a phone as seems to have happened, and putting material of this nature on the internet without consent, are crimes we'll investigate. Do you have any idea who might be involved in these crimes?"

"None, I'm afraid. So many students were engaged with social media it's impossible to determine who the ringleader might be."

"We have a Cyber Investigations unit we'll pass this onto. Is Lucy Ryan in?"

"Her mother called to tell us that Lucy is sick."

"We'll see if we can talk with Lucy and that might help us. Is there anything else?"

"No, thank you Senior Constable Scott and Constable Hewson. I'll show you out."

Back in the car, Luke thought. "I'll speak with Cyber Investigations," he said. "Can you check Facebook, Twitter and Instagram to see if these pictures are still around, and if so put in a request to have them taken down?"

"Principal Mr McCaughan said clips too," Alice said. "Those might be on porn sites."

"Can you check those?"

"I'm not a big expert on that."

Luke wasn't going to admit anything of that nature! "Just type porn sites in Google and that will give you what you want."

"Yeah."

Back in the Operations Room, Luke took a desk to shortly be talking with Ben White of Cyber Investigations. The news wasn't good. Whoever posted material online would most likely have used a VPN which would make the source untraceable. If Luke connected the phone to his computer, Ben would match material on the phone to postings on all social media sites, but offered no guarantees. Luke connected the phone to his computer and therefore to the NSW Police network for Ben to do his thing. While that was happening. the other side of their investigation was more important.

"How's it going, Alice?" Luke asked.

"When the principal said personal and intimate, he wasn't joking!" Alice exclaimed. "Look at this."

Luke looked over Alice's shoulder at a clip of a well-proportioned young lady leaving nothing to the imagination. And then another clip even more explicit.

"Can you get those taken off social media?"

"I lodged requests for these two clips and a number of pictures. Now porn sites."

Alice did her Google search to link to a site: Pornhub.

"Now what?" Alice asked.

They had to search within a search.

"Can we check on everything posted yesterday?" Luke asked.

Alice frowned as she rummaged around the main page. "I can check on newest. No, better. I can check on newest based on duration."

"Do that and I'll do the same Google search for the next site on the list, whatever that is."

"Even if we find these clips and have them taken down, they're out there and will return."

"Yeah, I know."

"Luke," Alice said quietly.

He leaned close.

"At Lucy's age, certain feelings can be almost overpowering. In the past these feelings have resulted in unwanted teen pregnancies and other consequences."

"Boys this age have strong feelings too."

"Girls can do sexting quite aggressively."

"I'm not a girl so I don't know how it feels for a girl, but I understand what you're saying. In the past as you said, this was expressed privately rather than online."

"That is something we tend to discourage more than we should."

Luke didn't disagree, remembering how he felt at that age.

"I understand," Luke said to wrap that up. "We'll deal with what we can now, and see Lucy when we're finished."

Alice turned to her screen while Luke started on the next site where he also had the option to search by newest and duration.

"What are you two up to?" Leon asked.

Luke turned to face Leon. "Alice put in requests to have postings she identified taken down from social media. There are clips involved in this, so now we're checking porn sites. The girl is underage and it's a non-consensual posting of her material. When we've dealt with that, we'll speak with the girl."

"There's a boy, too," Alice said. "I found his pictures and clips on social media, probably sent to Lucy in reply. He's Glen Ward aged 19."

"Brother of Joshua Ward?" Luke asked.

"Glen Ward is the non-identical twin brother of Joshua Ward."

"We'll speak with Glen. He might have posted this, but that's unlikely given he wouldn't have needed to steal and discard Lucy Ryan's smartphone to do that."

"Agreed," Leon said. "I'll leave you to your searching."

Luke turned to his computer screen to continue his search, while thinking these clips and pictures will be around forever. Worse that Lucy Ryan was from a generation who knew that. She would have been told not to, but in the excitement of a moment her feelings took over from what she was told, as can happen. Harmless fun she would have thought, now gone badly for her.

* * *

Lucy lay on her bed and cried and cried and cried. Her mother hammered on her bedroom door.

"Lucy what's wrong?" Mum called through the door.

"Go away Mum!"

"You can't stay in your bedroom all day."

"Just go away."

Lucy put her head down to cry while hoping her pillow would muffle the noise of her sobs. She turned to her laptop: the messages! Slut, bitch, whore, if you were my bitch I'd fuck you good and hard, a disgrace to all women, I'll give you a good fucking that your boyfriends not giving you. Message after message after message of hate. Lucy closed her laptop and buried her head under her pillow.

* * *

Glen got texts from his friends and Instagram messages too. The content was always the same. Somehow their pictures and clips got out there with Lucy being treated particularly badly. Glen rang Lucy but her phone was switched off. He didn't want to go her house; that would be too awkward. For sure their relationship was over before it even started, but that was only a minor issue. The bigger issue was they, and particularly Lucy, were out there everywhere.

# Chapter Twenty Three

Luke put his cap on, and with Alice by his side he strode to 27 Trafalgar Street to knock on the front door. A middle-aged woman answered with her mouth hanging open.

"My name's Senior-Constable Scott of Young Police," Luke said while showing his warrant card, "and with me is Constable Hewson. I would like to speak with Lucy Ryan if that's possible."

"She's in her room; she's been there all day. What has she done?"

"This isn't about illegal activities that directly involve Lucy," Luke said, "but I would like to speak with her."

"Alright. My name's Dawn Ryan."

Luke noticed Alice recording that in her notebook as Mrs Ryan showed them into a bland, beige, neat, tidy and well-maintained home, to knock on a door in a corridor of doors.

"Lucy, the police are here to see you."

After a moment the door opened to reveal a well-proportioned teenage girl with red cheeks and puffy eyes. She wore long pyjamas.

"These are Senior-Constable Scott and Constable Hewson," Mrs Ryan said. "They would like to talk with you."

Lucy Ryan backed away to allow Luke and Alice to enter, before closing the door on her mother.

"I know why you're here," Lucy Ryan said.

"First things first," Luke said. "You did nothing illegal so you don't have to worry about that. Now, do you know who took your phone to get at your pictures and video clips?"

"I have no idea. Earlier that day I showed pictures of Glen, my boyfriend, to Kayla, Alana, Amy and Ann."

"What are their full names?" Luke asked.

"Kayla Brown, Alana Hayes, Amy Evans and Ann Smith."

Beside him, Alice wrote.

"Do you think any of your friends would have stolen your phone?"

"Unless it was random bad luck, it might have been one of my friends, or they told someone else."

"How are you feeling?" Alice asked.

"I feel terrible. It's gone everywhere and I've received terrible messages calling me things. I just did it because, well, I suppose we had a great date and I was happy."

Luke handed a Headspace card to Lucy Ryan.

"I recommend you go here to talk with their counsellor. She can help you with what you're going through. In the meantime, we'll attempt to track the person who stole your phone, but that won't necessarily be the person or persons who posted on social media and porn sites."

"Is this on porn sites too?" Lucy Ryan asked with her eyes wide.

"I'm afraid so. We've asked for the clips we've identified to be taken down because there hasn't been consent for posting, but that doesn't mean there aren't other copes we haven't been able to find, or doesn't prevent these clips being re-uploaded at a later date."

"They say such things will be around forever and it's true."

"Talk with the counsellor at Headspace and she can help you with strategies for dealing with this situation." Luke paused for that to sink in. "Is there anything else you want to tell us?"

"No, nothing I can think of. Thanks for coming."

Luke left Lucy Ryan while hoping she spoke with Chloe. Next was Glen Ward. At his address a haggard woman smoking and still in her nightie, answered the door. After greetings, Luke and Alice were in the bedroom of Glen Ward.

"First things first," Luke stated. "You've done nothing illegal so you don't have to worry about that."

"Really?" Glen Ward exclaimed, obviously surprised.

"The law has been changed to take into account the differences between privately-shared pictures and clips, and material of under-age participants produced under duress for financial or other gains."

"That's a relief but poor Lucy."

"Are you alright?" Alice asked.

"My pictures and clips haven't been shared as much, and I can deal with that anyway. My problem is we had great first date until this happened. This will be awkward for me now."

Luke gave Glen Ward a Headspace card. "These people can help you with this or other issues."

Glen Ward looked at the card. "I'll see them when I get a chance."

"Is there anything else you want to tell us?"

"I can't think of anything. I'm just feeling bad for Lucy, although neither of us intended any harm."

"Thank you, Glen. We'll leave now."

Outside at the car, Luke pondered. "Back to the school to interview...."

"Kayla Brown, Alana Hayes, Amy Evans and Ann Smith," Alice said as she looked at her notebook. "They won't tell us, will they?"

"No they won't, while fingerprints on a well-used smartphone will be either impossible to lift or easy to explain away. But we have to do this."

"To close this case."

"Yeah."

Luke took his cap off to get into their car. He hoped Lucy took his advice about seeing Headspace.

* * *

She was young, voluptuous for her age, beautiful and instantly recognisable.

"Hi," she said. "I'm Lucy Ryan."

"Hi Lucy, I'm Chloe. Please take a seat."

Lucy sat on the couch with Chloe beside.

"What can I do for you, Lucy?"

"Well," Lucy said while staring into space. "We've been told not to sext but I thought it would be safe with my new boyfriend, but my phone was stolen and now it's gone viral on Instagram and Facebook. I did a couple of clips and I've been told they're now on porn sites."

Chloe had seen them. "Unfortunately what's done is done and can't be undone, but this is a short-tem setback more than anything else."

"People hate me and wrote I was a slut and worse. Some wanted to kill me even."

"Our society doesn't treat women well when it comes to sexual desires and sexual behaviours. If a man did the same thing, calling them names and making death threats wouldn't be a part of it."

"There were clips by my boyfriend with more like congratulations."

"I won't ever recommend making and sending explicit pictures and clips, but I do congratulate you, Lucy, for expressing your sexual desires in such a way."

She momentarily twinged a smile. "That's why I did it. I wanted to share myself with Glen."

"If people have a problem with a woman who's in tune with her sexual power, that's their problem and not your problem. Hold your head high, Lucy, even if they call you names, and it will fade in time."

"Do I have sexual power?"

"All women have sexual power, and on that day you chose to use your power."

"Yes, I did."

"What are you doing at the moment?" Chloe asked.

"Mostly staying in my room, except for now, but I have to get back to school. This is why I came here."

"Do you have a friend who can support you, so you're not alone when you go back to school?"

"Yes I do."

"Now you know what you should do."

"She lives with her boyfriend, everyone knows, but she's not called a slut."

"Our society expects women to be sexually chaste. Your friend living with her boyfriend is sexually monogamous in a long-term relationship that's close to being married."

"Ah, yes, I understand. Single women are sluts while married women are acceptable."

"That's the expectation but reality is different, of course."

"If this mess didn't happen, eventually I would have gone further with Glen even though we don't live together."

"Most young women have boyfriends, which is fine as long as they don't flaunt their sexual selves."

"Men can."

"This is why you shouldn't be ashamed but proud. You showed what women actually feel and do."

"That's right."

"Now, your boyfriend."

"I don't know if I can – you know. Just getting back to school is going to be hard."

"I understand. One step at a time."

"Yeah. If this blows over, maybe."

"Ignore their insults and they will get bored soon enough."

"You're right." Lucy stood. "Now I have a friend to ring and support to arrange."

Chloe stood. "Thank you for coming here, Lucy. Come back to talk with me, anytime."

Chloe watched her go. Chloe felt sad that a simple expression of sexual desire turned tragic. She hoped in time Lucy and her boyfriend had a future together, but more than likely they didn't. The worst outcome would be self-harm or even suicide, as sometimes happens. Chloe hoped Lucy had the support she needed to get over the worst of this.

* * *

Sophie's mobile vibrated with an incoming call which was odd. Mostly people texted. She picked it up to see Lucy calling.

"Hi Lucy," Sophie greeted.

"Hi Sophie; I suppose you know what happened."

"Yeah I do. Are you alright?"

"Not really but I'll survive. I put it out there, didn't I?"

"You sure did; that was hot!"

"Really?"

Sophie looked around to spot nobody in hearing range. "Hands up any woman who's not done that to herself. But to share that with your boyfriend! That would have kept him satisfied for weeks."

Silence for a moment. "I wish more were like you," Lucy eventually said. "The reason I rang is to ask you to be my support person for a few days."

"Of course," Sophie said even though she was supporting Emma, who actually didn't need support these days. Sophie had an idea. "Meet me at the corner of Ripon Street, fifteen minutes before nine. We'll enter school together."

"That's a great idea." Silence. "Would you have done that if you weren't living together?"

"I might have," Sophie said even though she wouldn't in a million years. "But I do know it can go sour."

"Yeah I know. You're speaking to the biggest slut in Young, you know."

"No I'm not; I'm speaking to my best friend."

"Thanks Sophie."

Lucy ended the call while Sophie felt sad for her friend. On Saturday night Lucy and Glen had a future, but probably not now. Sophie also felt sad for Glen who was a nice guy, except nice guys came last in life. She thought there was a saying like that; if there was that saying was right.

## Chapter Twenty Four

There was Lucy waiting as Sophie closed.

"Hi," Lucy said shyly.

"Hi Lucy," Sophie said firmly. "Let's show them!"

Sophie slipped her arm inside Lucy's arm, to arm-in-arm stride towards the gates, through into the grounds, ignoring abuse and jeers. Arm-in-arm all the way to their lockers, still ignoring every insult imaginable. Year 12, both 16; they were older and stronger. They were old enough and strong enough to wear down petty, small-minded schoolchildren.

## Chapter Twenty Five

Chloe had just made tea when she heard someone in the shop. She went there, mug in hand, to see Emma from a few weeks ago, absolutely sparkling.

"Hi Emma," Chloe greeted. "How are you?"

"Hi Chloe," Emma greeted. "I told you I would come here to tell you I'm clean, and now I'm clean."

"How long has it been?"

"Two weeks and three days, but I haven't craved for four days."

"This is a great effort!"

"With help from my friends."

"Are your plans for your future the same?"

"I like what I do."

"I can see that, so good for you."

"I do intend to study for later," Emma said. "Distance learning from TAFE NSW for a Certificate Four in Health Administration. I'm a country girl, and I want a qualification which enables me to work in the country. This one will; I'm sure."

Chloe knew that qualification would.

"I have free time during my days," Emma said, "so this certificate and my work will be good for me."

"Do you have friends for support?"

"I have many friends. Some friends know everything: those who helped me and a school friend who's a regular client," and Emma laughed. "And other great friends."

"Even though you're clean now, cravings can return days, weeks, months, and even years into the future. To some extent this is a lifetime issue."

"But if I'm satisfied in my life, and busy, that's better?"

"Yes it is. You don't need a relationship to be satisfied, Emma. If you have a good relationship that's fine, but if you're happy in other ways that's fine too."

"That's how I feel at the moment. I'm free, independent, I have many good friends, but I'll keep an open mind about a man for my life."

"Good. Anytime you want to talk about problems or just anything, please call by."

"I just came here to thank you, Chloe, for pointing me in the right direction."

"Thank you Emma."

She left with Chloe feeling warm all over. Successes like Emma made her career more than worthwhile.

* * *

Emma put the bag of groceries on her kitchen counter when her work phone rang. She fished through her shoulder bag to smile as he noticed the contact; she made contacts of her regular clients.

"Hello," Emma said in her professional voice.

"Hi Emma, this is James.  Are you feeling better?"

"Hi James; I'm feeling much better."

"Can I see you?"

"You can see me anytime."

"Half an hour?'

Always half an hour!  "Half an hour will be fine."

"See you then."

He ended the call.  Emma put milk and cheese in her fridge, checked if her water jug had enough, which it did, and she put the bread in her pantry cupboard.  She went to her bedroom to undress, put her clothes folded in her wardrobe for later; then went to her bathroom to quickly shower.  After drying, back to her bedroom where, in her work drawer she selected her black bikini; one of the bikinis she wore to greet her clients, before sitting to buckle her black stilettos.  She checked herself in the mirror on the back of the wardrobe door, hair fine, bikini fine, and now she knew guys liked her figure.

The buzzer rang.  Emma opened the door where James was dressed in jeans and a t-shirt as always, freshly showered with damp hair so he didn't have to shower at Emma's and eat into his hour, but this time holding a bunch of flowers. How sweet!

"Hi Emma, this is for you," James said as he handed them across.

"Thank you James," Emma gushed as she kissed his cheek; that was a lovely thought. "Come inside and I'll find a vase."

Emma's parents had boxes of household items from when her granny had to go to a nursing home. Emma was given the lot which gave her almost everything she needed for her home, including a vase. Dressed in stilettos, that vase on a top shelf in her kitchen was reachable too. She took it down, half-filled it with water, then laid the flowers on her counter to untie a red bow and unroll white and purple striped paper.

"How have you been?" Emma asked James.

"Same old, same old. And you now?"

"I'm much better thank you."

"You look good."

Emma smiled at that as she took her scissors from a drawer to cut string around the bunch. Then she arranged them in the vase – nice. She put the vase at the end of her counter.

"I'll leave these pretty flowers here for when I'm cooking and eating," she said. "Do you want a glass of water?"

"Yes please."

He always did.

"Oh this," he said, as he pulled out four, 50 dollar notes which Emma popped part-under the vase. She then poured two glasses of water from her jug, gave one to James, before taking his hand for the walk to her bedroom. There she put her glass beside his glass on her bedside cabinet, before hugging him, and he hugged her while untying her bikini top. James liked undressing Emma, but always left her stilettos on, before he hugged and kissed her in bed, oral on her which he didn't know how to do, a condom, and then missionary or cowgirl. Later she would massage him. He was sweet, no question, but Emma didn't like sweet, except in clients. The man for her was nice like Josh, not bad boys, but nice men with a bit of edge to them, like Josh too. Not Glen; despite being a twin he lacked that edge of his brother. By then James had untied Emma's bikini bottom, so she followed his lead to her bed. There after a bit more hugging and kissing he slid down for Emma to pretend, and even though he didn't really know how she felt her arousal building. One day she might show James how to take her all the way, instead of dealing with herself after he left. But sweet was good, and sex was always nice even if it wasn't expert, and there were worse ways to spend an hour on a Wednesday afternoon.

## Chapter Twenty Six

Daniel overheard Lisa talking to a familiar, gruff voice.

"Daniel!" Lisa called. "Franco's here!"

Daniel strolled to the front door to shake hands. "Hi Franco."

"Hello Daniel," Franco said with his face far from happy.

"Come through; I was practicing pool. Want something to drink?"

"I'm fine."

They went to the pool room where the always smartly-casually dressed Franco Romano, early 60s, stocky build with a full head of grey hair, and of Italian background from the Griffith Mafia, stopped just inside the doorway with his arms crossed on his barrel-like chest.

"You have a fine home, Daniel," Franco said. "Big debts maybe?"

Daniel gathered balls to rack them up. "Maybe," Daniel eventually said.

"It would be in your interest to increase turnover, wouldn't it?"

"I've got feedback that the stuff Bishop sells is good, better than yours, which is why he's doing so well." Daniel brought his cue down, lined it up and did a shot to spread balls to the four corners of the table.

"My stuff is good."

"Young is small, Franco, and word is out there. Bishop has better stuff."

"Yeah, well, when you make your next payment on this mansion, think about how your efforts could close the gap."

Daniel lined his shot to in-off the white ball! He stood straight to stare down Franco who was unmoved and who was right. He had debts and was struggling to pay them.

"I'll see what I can do," Daniel said.

"That's what I like to hear."

In reality with Bishop having better stuff, cheaper prices, and Josh Ward and his partner's girl Sophie cornering the youth market, Daniel knew he couldn't do much.

"See you Daniel."

"See you Franco."

Franco left while Daniel decided to abandon his practice for a game he never played against anyone else, on a too-expensive table in a big room that was barely used. Instead Daniel went to the study, originally a fourth bedroom, to sit at the desk and stare at Lisa's spreadsheet on the laptop, but the numbers in her budget didn't make any sense. Then we went through bills in the basket: so many. Water, gas, electricity, rates: more than a thousand dollars! He went back to the spreadsheet.

"Gazing at it won't make it better," Lisa said from the doorway.

Daniel rotated the chair to look at Lisa.

"Look it's almost seven. Let's watch Netflix.

That was another bill sucking him dry but they paid for it so he might as wall watch it.

"You choose," Lisa said as she flopped into a cream-coloured leather armchair. Not just leather but the softest, most supple, most expensive leather in the shop. Daniel scrolled the movie guide while dismissing those he'd already seen, until a new one caught his eye: American Dreamer released in September. *'A down on his luck rideshare driver who makes extra cash chauffeuring a low-level drug dealer around town, finds himself in a serious financial bind and decides to kidnap the dealer's child'*. Interesting. Daniel sat down to watch what he was sure to be an interesting movie.

# Chapter Twenty Seven

Daniel watched from Lisa's Lexus parked opposite and just along from Jack Bishop's dump. *How could anyone live in such a shithole?* For sure Bishop didn't pay much rent on that place. But that wasn't why Daniel was there. Lisa mentioned Bishop's partner's girl Sophie, and she was why Daniel was there. After that movie on Saturday evening, the pieces fell into place for Daniel. He had the where, he had some leverage to make the where part of it happen, and he knew a way to keep those bikies out of it. All he needed was the how, and like in the movie the girl's routine would give him that. That Monday morning for her regular weekday routine. Now Daniel waited for a girl around Josh's age, 18 or 19, in order to follow her to work or wherever. The front door opened, a girl emerged and she was gorgeous! In a Young High School uniform so somewhat younger than Josh, the lucky young man. Daniel watched Sophie walk along the street; it was about a 20 minute walk to the high school. After all it was safe to walk to school in Young. Daniel couldn't help but smile as that thought crossed his mind, while he pulled out to follow Sophie at a distance.

* * *

The younger children still raced out the gate and it was only older girls who walked properly. These days Sophie, Lucy and Hannah were three friends together. Since the stolen smartphone episode and the near-catastrophe that came from that, not fully abated by any means, Sophie didn't trust Lucy's former friends, nor did Lucy although she never said that directly. As forecast, that windy, cloudy day already drizzled light rain for expected heavy rain late tomorrow. If so that would be a good follow-up from heavy rain a week ago. Being drizzly and one of Josh's days off from Mitre 10, she expected to see him waiting, which he was.

"There's Josh," Sophie said. "Looks like I have a ride."

"Lucky you," Lucy said.

"Can you give me a lift?" Hannah asked.

"Yeah, sure," Sophie agreed on Josh's behalf.

Sophie wondered then thought: *why not?*

"Did you ever catch up with Glen?" Sophie asked Lucy.

"It's a bit awkward."

"I know Glen; he's a nice guy. It wasn't your fault, and if you catch up with him I know he'll be cool."

"I'll think about it. See you Sophie and Hannah."

"See you Lucy," they said in near-unison.

Sophie ran to Josh to kiss him before throwing her backpack on the backseat; then stopping. She remembered that funny feeling she had that morning. She was certain someone was following her but all she saw that morning was a dark blue car, new and shining, driven by a man wearing sunglasses. Sophie looked all around until saw that same car again, and again the man with sunglasses. Odd, especially sunglasses on a cloudy and wet afternoon.

"Are you alright?" Josh said.

"What? No, I'm fine."

"How much rain is coming, do you reckon?" Josh asked.

"I hope lots."

"How are you, Hannah?" Josh asked as she climbed into the back of his car.

"We need lots of rain, don't we?"

"We do."

Josh started his car and drove away.

* * *

Sophie's walk to school was almost due south along Blackett Avenue, across the town centre and further south to the high school. Daniel watched Sophie on Tuesday where she left home at the same time, to plan for Wednesday. He walked the route later on Tuesday where the best spot was not far south of her house, at the intersection with Melville Street. All Daniel needed was a few minutes with no passers-by and for sure his plan would work.

Rain started that night; heavy as forecast but heavier than Daniel expected as it pounded his tiled roof. The rain the other week was only a start and for sure Young and the region needed more rain, but for Daniel rain made his plan somewhat uncertain. If Sophie was driven to school the next morning all his preparations were for nothing. Fuck, of course Josh would drive Sophie to school! And after school he would pick her up, all the more certain as rain was forecast

207

to last for a few days. Daniel sighed, but rain would pass as it always did. He just had to be patient.

## Chapter Twenty Eight

Sophie went to the kitchen where she switched on the kettle before spooning Nescafe into two mugs along with sugar, while in the background the shower ran noisily. She grabbed a bowl to pour Nutri Grain and milk. She sat at the small table to eat before the kettle switched off just as Josh came into the room. He made coffee and gave her one. Sophie drank while Josh poured Nutri Grain and milk into a bowl.

"Do you want a lift to school?" he asked.

"How's the weather?" Sophie asked.

Josh looked out the window. "Cloudy but dry," he said.

"I'll walk."

"Are you sure?"

"I like the walk."

Josh joined her at the table.

"How's your friend?" Jessica asked from the doorway.

"She's recovered now," Sophie said.

"That's good to hear. I'm proud of you, Sophie, and you've been great Josh." Jessica came to lean against the kitchen cabinet. "Sophie pointed out some hypocrisy on my part which I couldn't deny, so her room became your space. A few times Josh, you had meals with us where we got to know you better, when Sophie wanted the next step. I thought you were a good guy, someone who was good for Sophie, so here you are. Now you're being good to an ex-girlfriend, isn't it?"

209

"We're still friends," Josh said.

"You're a good guy Josh. Are you walking, Sophie?"

"Yes Mum; I should go. See you."

"See you Sophie."

Sophie headed out on a cloudy-dark day but dry, and forecast to remain cloudy and dry. It was good of Mum to ask after Emma who was recovered, more through willpower than anything Josh and Sophie could do for her, and working again, although Sophie didn't like that. Sophie's ex Jason watched too much porn, and Mum had already warned Sophie that some guys were like that. Jason wanted Sophie to shave, but she wasn't going to turn herself into a girl just because porn stars did that. Then Jason wanted to fuck Sophie's arse which she refused to do; instead he pulled out of her to spray her face which was terrible. She told him not to do that again but he did, and fucking with Jason seemed like being used so she told they were finished. Later, Josh was totally good in bed as he was with everything else. Close, connected, not so serious and even fun. But Emma? Fucking for money? Sophie didn't like the thought of that; but they all weren't poured from the same mould, were they?

Sophie walked along Blackett Avenue with everything muddy around her. Over 110 millimetres so far that month was what farmers and Young, and especially firefighters, needed.

* * *

Daniel couldn't believe his luck as she approached in her uniform: tall, slender, leggy, long blonde hair: definitely Sophie. He felt for the syringe in his left pocket and the syringe in his right pocket before looking around, but on a dreary morning in the poorer part of Young, nobody moved except one girl in a school uniform. Daniel retreated further into Melville Street until he saw Sophie pass. Daniel pulled his balaclava down before he stepped out to follow her, with big strides to quickly catch her.

"Sophie!" Daniel called and she spun around for Daniel to stab her arse and press the syringe of fentanyl with his thumb. Into muscle as he read.

"Fuck!" Sophie swore as she tried to pull away but Daniel held onto her tightly. She squirmed against him, but less and less until she was nearly limp. Daniel dragged her; now almost totally limp, to the BMW, where with one hand he pressed the button on the tailgate. It opened automatically for Daniel to pick Sophie up by her shoulders, she was light, and sit her on the load area made bigger by the back seat folded flat, before pushing her down. When she was down he clipped her wrists with Lisa's sex toy handcuffs, stuffed a handkerchief into her mouth, took her bag and checked it for her smartphone, then took the other syringe, narcan, to stab her arse and press it with his thumb. Sophie lay unmoving while Daniel watched and waited. One minute, two minutes maybe; suddenly she came to and struggled, kicked her legs and tried to shout, but those handcuffs and the ad-hoc gag were good enough. Daniel stood behind the BMW to press the button for the tailgate to close. He got in front, buckled up, pressed the start button, to head north out Young. Past the suburbs, picking up speed, slowing for Cowra then picking up speed again, before turning onto an unmarked track, muddy after days of rain. Slow now; even though Daniel had four wheel drive that wasn't a panacea for potholes full of water. On and on until he stopped at one of the Cliefden Caves, now closed-off with a gate, chain and padlock.

Daniel pressed the button on his armrest before climbing out to the now open tailgate. He grabbed the boltcutters lying beside Sophie.

"How are you my sweet little Sophie?" Daniel asked, to which she kicked and bucked and tried to probably swear. At the gate Daniel sliced the chain to open it wide.

The most difficult part was getting Sophie the few metres from the BMW into the cave, given she used every muscle in her body to resist him, but even though Daniel wasn't that fit, a schoolgirl stood no chance. Eventually she was in the cave, gag removed and swearing quite colourfully as Daniel used a new chain and a new padlock to lock her securely. He took the old chain and padlock to the back of the BMW, returned to the highway, drove a few hundred metres, then turned onto the mud of O'Brien's Road and then onto his parent's driveway. That was just as rough and muddy as the track to the cave. He pulled up, removed his balaclava but left it in the glovebox, before walking to their front door and ringing the bell.

Dad answered.

"Hi Dad," Daniel said with his hand on the keys in his pocket. "We need to talk."

"I was going to check our tank anyway."

They crossed the muddy yard.

"You remember the cave we used to play in when we were young?" Daniel said.

"Yeah I remember it," Dad said. "It's locked now."

Daniel took out two keys on a ring. "This is the key for that cave. In it you'll find a girl, about 16, with handcuffs. You have the key for those too. Feed her."

"Why am I going to do this?"

"Because you owe me a lot of money, and you need that money to keep flowing because it's going to take more than 110 millimetres of rain to keep this place afloat. You know where my money comes from, but this girl is stopping my business which stops this farm; doesn't it?"

"How can you lock up a 16 year old girl?"

"It'll only be for a few days. Once her family agrees to leave Young, I'll take her home."

Dad glared at Daniel before snatching the keys.

"Alright but never again," Dad growled. "And don't tell your mother!"

"How will you get food to her without Mum knowing?"

"I'll think of a way. A few days you say?"

"If someone took Amy when she was 16, you would have done anything to get her back, wouldn't you?"

"What if they call the police?"

"They're dealing so they won't."

Dad shook his head.

"See ya Dad," Daniel said casually.

Dad stood, arms crossed, glaring, while Daniel climbed into his muddy BMW for the drive home. His BMW was a mess; he'd call into the carwash on the way.

## Chapter Twenty Nine

Josh sat on the bonnet of his car, although it wasn't wet. Simply he wasn't working that day so he decided to pick Sophie up. He spotted Hannah and Lucy but not Sophie. Hannah came to Josh.

"Hi Josh," she greeted. "Sophie didn't come to school today."

"Pardon?" Josh asked. "No, I heard. Has anyone heard from her?"

"We haven't heard a thing."

Josh pulled out his phone, pressed her contact for it to ring and ring before going to voicemail. Odd.

"Sophie's not answering?" Hannah asked.

"She's not," Josh said.

"I hope she's alright."

"Me too." Josh thought. He had to see Jessica and Jack. "I'll speak with her parents now. See you Hannah."

"See you Josh."

Josh drove home, totally unfocussed, to turn into their driveway where he noticed an envelope in the letterbox, which was odd given Jessica brought their mail in earlier that day. It wasn't an envelope but A4 paper, thick and wrinkly, folded in half and stapled. Josh paused to think how to break this to Jessica and Jack. He went inside where they were in the living room, fan running, and Jessica by the open window smoking. Josh stood inside the doorway with the paper in his hands.

"I have this," Josh said, "which might explain why Sophie wasn't at school today, and why Hannah hasn't seen or heard from her."

Jessica snatched the page, tore it apart and read it. "Fuck!" she exclaimed.

Jessica handed it to Jack who read before handing it to Josh. It was a note made of newspaper words and letters pasted to a page. *'Get out of town and Sophie will return. Police or bikies and Sophie will not return.'*

"Who do you think?" Jack asked.

Josh knew. "I don't know Mike Kelly that well," he said, "but I do know Daniel Stewart is stupid enough to try this."

"What do you mean try?" Jessica said before smoking furiously. "They have Sophie so we don't have a choice. Money isn't worth Sophie's life."

"Agreed," Jack said, "although I don't want scum like Stewart to get away with this."

"That's why Daniel Stewart is stupid," Josh said. "You agree to leave Young and he gives Sophie back, and maybe you leave. But when Sophie's safe, who knows?"

Jack chuckled. "Yes, you're right."

"I don't want to interrupt Sophie's school in her most important year," Jessica said. "Regardless of what we have to do, I would prefer to stay here."

216

Jack frowned. "This is like those fake drive-bys," he said. "If the police get wind of this we might get dragged into it. We'll take our drugs to the storage unit, including personal supplies."

"You know we're only once a fortnight," Josh said.

"And then you – afterwards!" Jack exclaimed

"That's my daughter you're talking about," Jessica said while she butted her cigarette in the ashtray on the former mantel of the former fireplace.

"You know I love her," Josh said.

"I know you do, and she loves you."

"We'll get her back," Jack said. "Clean this place out now and then we'll work out how to prove we're leaving for good."

Josh knew. "He or someone he knows will watch for a furniture moving truck."

"Yeah, you're right."

"You two clean up and I'll book Allied Pickfords," Jessica said.

They never kept much in the house, just enough for a day or two, and always in the same place. Josh went to help Jack more to keep himself occupied and not worry about Sophie.

* * *

Sophie had never felt so – shitty. It was cold in that cave, too cold for her summer uniform, and movement was difficult with handcuffs on. She knew who it was – Daniel Stewart.

Despite the cold Sophie was thirsty, and after quite a few hours her stomach rumbled too. Fuck – how long was she going to be there? Sophie heard the crunch of tyres on gravel and then a diesel engine. She looked out to see an old, white ute pull up where the engine rattled to a stop. A tall, older man in a broad-brim Akubra farmer's hat, chequered long-sleeve shirt and jeans; face darkened and creased by many years of sun, emerged from the ute to walk in farmer's boots to the gate, where he used a key to enter the cave. Sophie watched as he carried a pizza box.

"I'm told you'll only be here for a few days," he said in a deep, gruff voice.

Sophie nodded her head but there was something else. "Can you take these handcuffs off, please? With the gate locked I'm not going anywhere."

"Yeah, alright."

He put the pizza box down before bending down with two keys on a ring in his big, roughened hands. He unlocked those sex-toy handcuffs but effective nonetheless.

"I brought something to eat but it'll be a bit cold."

"I need something to drink," Sophie said, now beyond being polite to her jailer.

"I have water in the ute."

He strode out of the cave while Sophie ate half-cold mozzarella and parsley pizza which was an odd choice. He handed her a half-empty bottle of water which Sophie drank greedily, before eating more pizza before it got stone cold.

"Is there anything else you need?" he asked.

"I need somewhere to shit," Sophie said.

"I can't help you with that, except this cafe is big and nobody will see you."

"I need toilet paper."

"I'll bring some next time."

Sophie ate more pizza until she was full.

"I'll be back tomorrow," he said.

"Don't you want to know my name?"

"I don't want to be part of this."

"My name's Sophie, I'm 16, and you're part of this."

He locked the gate before climbing into his ute and driving away.

# Chapter Thirty

Josh hardly slept. Their bed was a constant reminder to get Sophie back. Josh hoped Daniel treated Sophie well in the meantime. Josh briefly wondered if Daniel's partner Lisa was involved but decided she wasn't.

After showering, Josh went to the kitchen to make coffee and have something to eat, despite not feeling that hungry. As always Jack had his ancient transistor radio tuned to ABC for the 8am news bulletin. Josh sat at the small table to eat Nutri Grain and drink coffee as the music played. Headline stories were about fires now mostly extinguished, and a schoolgirl gone missing on her way to Young High School. *Fuck!*

They knew everything: her age, her friends being worried, the only thing they didn't mention was her name. But for sure that was Sophie. Jack switched his radio off.

"One of Sophie's friends has told radio stations," Josh said. "They didn't know that makes things worse for her."

"It could have been your sister."

"It could have been but Sophie has quite a few friends."

"The police will be onto this," Jack said. "They'll think it's strange we didn't tell them."

Josh thought: the note made from newspapers was like from a movie, and probably didn't have fingerprints because Daniel wore latex gloves like they do in moves. What else from movies?

"She's done this before and always comes home," Josh said.

"Fuck, great idea Josh!"

Josh finished his coffee before pulling out his phone. He scrolled his contacts and pressed.

"Hi Josh," Hannah greeted.

"Hi Hannah. Did you hear?"

"It was on Rocky FM."

"Do you know what's going on with us here?" Josh asked.

"I'm not that naive!"

"Does Mum know?"

"She is that naive."

"When I hear something about Sophie I'll let you know."

"Thanks Josh."

Josh ended the call.

"It wasn't Hannah and it was also on Rocky FM," Josh told Jack, while he heard Jessica assembling cardboard cartons in the living room for their move in two days time, with the tearing sound of packing tape over and over. Josh took one of those cartons to pack their belongings including Sophie tight denim shorts, perhaps the shorts she wore the day she stole his heart, and other clothes more for winter: tight jeans, tight yoga pants which didn't suit many women but would suit her, and a few pairs of non-school slacks, which would have been tight knowing Sophie.

Knocking at the door which Josh heard Jessica answer. Before long Josh heard an argument between Jessica and a woman; he poked his head into the corridor to see Jessica shoving a well-dressed woman in a light grey suit through the door, literally shoving her, and locking it.

"Fuck, television!" Jessica exclaimed before reaching for her cigarettes.

Josh went into the living room for Jessica to grab him. "Careful," she said.

Josh understood. Instead he stood by the living room window to ease his head around the corner to see a parked, white SUV with the Prime, Orange logo on the side, a local news reporter he recognised, Jennifer Davies, a man with a camera on his shoulder, and another man holding a boom microphone over Davies while she spoke towards the camera.

Josh sat with his back to the wall while contemplating how far this had gone.

"What do you think, mate?" Jack asked while Jessica smoked furiously in the corridor.

"You two should talk to them. That story – sometimes she does this."

"But she doesn't, and if they talk to her friends or the school in Wagga they'll find that out soon enough."

"Well then, you're worried, you don't know anything and you hope she comes home safe and sound. If you don't say anything it'll look odd."

"He's right," Jessica said before she crossed the room to butt her cigarette.

Josh carefully peered out the window to see another white SUV, but with the ABC logo, now parked. A reporter, again a woman but in black slacks and a white blouse, this time holding a big, fluffy microphone, was joined by a cameraman who had a camera on his shoulder.

"The ABC is here," Josh said flatly.

"She's never done this before, we're worried, we don't know anything and we hope she comes home safe and sound," Jessica repeated. "I'm her mother and Jack is her step-father. Good – let's do this."

Josh put his head around the corner to watch two reporters, two cameramen and one sound recorder, swarm across their now greening grass. The crews and reporters stood side-by-side which was useful: killing two birds with one stone. After about 20 minutes, Jack and Jessica came inside.

"What's Daniel Stewart going to think when he sees this on the news?" Jessica asked before she lit another cigarette.

"I think his partner Lisa might be asking questions," Josh said.

"You're right about that."

\* \* \*

Luke had just turned onto the Olympic Way when their radio called 'Young 313', which Alice answered.

"Can you check on this missing schoolgirl?" Sally asked.

"On our way."

"Acknowledged."

Alice chuckled. "It's a bit embarrassing after hearing this story on the radio," she said.

It was. Luke drove through the town centre to the high school to park where it was again eerily quiet with students in class, as Luke reacquainted himself and Alice to the receptionist. Not long after they once more were in the office of the principal, Paul McCaughan, still overlooking an empty, asphalt assembly area. Alice already had her notebook out. Luke and Alice stood facing a peculiarly clean desk while Mr McCaughan stood behind his desk.

"Principal McCaughan," Luke began. "I believe there's a student who's gone missing."

"No report has been made but a year 12 student, Sophie Weaver, has failed to attend these past two days. Her mother hasn't contacted us."

Luke remembered interviewing Sophie Weaver after those unresolved drive-by shootings. This was no coincidence.

"Do you know if her classmates have heard from her?" Luke asked.

"I asked her English teacher to ask this question, where nobody has heard from Sophie. Some of Sophie's classmates are worried."

Luke took out a card. "If you hear anything about Sophie Weaver or if she shows up, can you call us at Young Police?" Luke asked as he handed the card across.

"I will, Senior Constable Scott."

"Thank you."

They headed to the car.

"Can you radio a report to VKG?" Luke asked.

"Sophie Weaver going missing isn't a coincidence," Alice said.

"No it's not, but until we get a missing persons from her mother we can't do a lot."

"That's true."

Luke climbed behind the wheel of 313 while thinking that Young now had a drug war on its hands.

* * *

"What the fuck have you been doing, Daniel?" Lisa called.

Daniel looked up from Facebook on his iPhone. "What is it?" he asked.

Lisa came into the room. "A schoolgirl has gone missing, Sophie Weaver, daughter of Jack Bishop and Jessica Weaver. It was on Prime News: interviews with Jack and Jessica and a picture of Sophie Weaver."

Daniel dropped his phone which clattered noisily when it hit ceramic tiles.

"I thought this would get them out of town and fix our problems," Daniel said quietly.

225

"Fuck Daniel!"

"But it could!"

"Where is Sophie – no. Don't tell me. If this goes to shit I'm leaving you for good, and taking the girls and half your shit too."

"You can take half of our debts."

"So your plan is they go, you give them Sophie, and then those bikies come to congratulate you?"

"Yeah – no, I hadn't thought of that."

"Well you should have!"

Lisa stomped off while Daniel now felt sick in his stomach. Achingly sick.

# Chapter Thirty One

ABC News was an hour after Prime where the story was somewhat less melodramatic, in the style of a government broadcaster. But as the reporter talked they had the same picture of Sophie, smiling in her uniform after passing Year 11 in Wagga. The loud music of his ZZ Top ringtone, one of Jacks quirky obsessions, shattered the silence. Jack took his ancient Galaxy smartphone from a pocket in his shorts.

"Hi Trev," Jack greeted then listened. "Daniel Stewart for sure." More listening. "He sent a note pasted from a newspaper like in a movie, where he wants us to leave town and he doesn't want police or bikies involved." A lot more listening. "Are you sure?" Listening. "She's 16, Trev." More listening. "I understand." Jack put his phone on the table and sighed.

"Trev and the guys saw this. He knows this is an extension of the fake drive-bys, of course. He's going to deal with it."

Jessica was smoking again. "That will put Sophie in danger," she said.

"We've exceeded expectations which Trev puts down to Josh and Sophie, and he doesn't want to lose what we've achieved."

Josh realised they'd been too good, if there was such a thing.

"When will they be here?" Jessica asked.

227

"Soon," Jack said.

"They'll beat the shit out of Daniel Stewart until he tells them where Sophie is."

"They're also going to take Mike Kelly in case he knows something."

"Do you think they'll kill Stewart over what he did?"

Jack shrugged his shoulders. "We just need to get Sophie back and then we'll be fine."

"What happens when Josh and Sophie go to Wagga to study?" Jessica asked.

"You've got your regular users now," Josh said. "If you need it I'll recruit a – girl preferably, for Saturday night parties. I mean, a quarter-share of what she sells will be lucrative." Josh thought Charlotte would be interested: she was a party girl and a regular customer already.

Jessica smoked and nodded her head. "If you do study business, Josh, you'll be good at that," she said. "If Trev saw this story, that means it was broadcast in Sydney. I'm sure the police here will be paying us a visit, when they get their shit together. We're clean of drugs in case they search, and the story is what we said in the interview. We know nothing."

"They won't believe that," Josh said.

"I don't give a fuck if they do or they don't; just don't stray from the script."

Jessica lit another cigarette while Josh went to their room to get away from her smoke haze, but there he didn't have a clue what to do. Wait for the police to come knocking, he supposed. Then he thought play against himself in Resident Evil 3. That would pass the time for a few hours.

* * *

Chloe turned the TV off before sipping her white wine while thinking.

"Young has become a hot-spot for crime," she eventually said.

"There are things I shouldn't say," Luke said. "Clearly there's a war going on between drug dealers."

"A schoolgirl though...." She thought. "You know I want to decriminalise drugs to minimise harm, put law enforcement money into rehab for the percentage who become addicted, and I suppose end drive-bys and kidnappings."

"What percentage becomes addicted?" Luke asked.

"Depends on the drug."

"Methamphetamine?"

"Methamphetamine addiction is 20.4 percent of users."

"Really?"

"You think drug use equals addiction, don't you?"

"Yeah, well...."

Chloe held her glass in front of her face. "Alcohol is a legal drug."

"What about alcohol addiction? What percentage?"

"Alcohol addiction is about 7 percent of those who drink; the same as gamblers who become addicted to gambling."

"Sex addiction?"

Chloe laughed. "Now that's controversial! You and I could make love every day, or even twice a day, and yet that's just – love, not addiction. I would say that if someone's life is being harmed by sex, say financially by seeing escorts all the time or losing their job through looking at porn on the internet at work, then that's harmful and needs help."

"No sex addiction then?"

"Sex that's harmful to the individual yet he or she can't stop could be considered an addiction."

"Not a husband and wife making love?"

Chloe finished her wine and put the empty glass down. "Is that a proposition?" she asked.

Luke stood so Chloe stood, for him to scoop her into his arms and carry her into their bedroom. There he laid her on their bed before unbuttoning his shirt.

## Chapter Thirty Two

Jennifer wheeled her Nissan X-Trail into the carpark of Prime, grabbed her shoulder bag, and slid out to press the remote to lock her compact SUV. She went inside where local television was friendly and in fact a joy to work in, but sadly on the way out. Only Prime and ABC now offered Central West and South-West Slopes news services: with Prime and ABC both based in Orange.

"Hi Jennifer," Tammy, the receptionist greeted.

"Hi Tammy."

"You're going to have a busy day."

"Has something happened?"

"You'll find out!"

Jennifer walked to the newsroom which was a hive of activity, all the more surprising given there were only four on the news team these days.

"Ah Jennifer!" Tamara, the news and local events manager, exclaimed. "There were multiple abductions in Young last night. I've sent you the emails we received from people there. Read them, and get yourself prepared to hit the road. All the details you need are in those emails."

"This might be an extension of those drive-bys and maybe even that girl gone missing," Jennifer said.

"Bikies were involved with last night's abductions so this is definitely an extension of those drive-by shootings. When you write your script, make the connection to the missing

231

schoolgirl a hypothetical possibility. She might have run off with a boyfriend or something like that."

"I'll do that," Jennifer said as he sat in her cubicle dominated by a laptop plugged into a big screen, but made personal with a picture of Jake and her 'Jennifer' coffee mug. After her laptop powered up, Jennifer was surprised by the numbers of emails: about two screens full. Jennifer read the first from 'John'.

'At about nine we heard cars drive up and doors slam, before we heard hammering on Daniel Stewart's front door across the road. I looked outside to see in the lights of Daniel's garden, six bikie-types dressed in leather jackets and jeans with patches I couldn't read from across the street. There was more hammering before they stood back to allow one bikie to smash down the front door with a sledgehammer. They all went inside and then three more came from the back of the house carrying Daniel between them. They put him in one of their cars, an SUV, and drove away.

Jennifer contemplated that. Some bikies went to the front door of Daniel Stewart's house while others went around the back, to abduct him when he tried to escape.

She went to the next email from Mary Mason which told something the same story but less precisely. John, whoever he was, was a typical man: straight down the line. The email after that was from Jason.

'At about 9.30 I heard shouting so looked outside to see three SUVs outside Mike Kelly's house. Bikie types in leather hammered on his door. They went inside, took Mike out and took him away.'

Jennifer browsed more emails but they were the same two events from different perspectives, except she found the three SUVs were 'dark'. So nine bikies arrived in SUVs, abducted Daniel Stewart after smashing his door and Stewart tried to escape, and shortly after abducted Mike Kelly peacefully by comparison. Jennifer quickly wrote her script along those lines. After pressing the print icon she pulled her work phone from her bag, scrolled her contacts and pressed one. It rang, he answered.

"Inspector Rogers, Young Police," he answered.

"Jennifer Davies, Prime News Orange," Jennifer replied. "We've received emails about two abductions yesterday evening in Young. Do you wish to comment?"

"Investigations on these abductions are ongoing and further information will be released in due course."

Jennifer expected that. "Do you believe these abductions are related to each other?"

"Our Investigations regarding these crimes are just starting."

"Come on Inspector Rogers; I have many witness accounts."

Silence for a moment. "It appears the same group of men abducted first Daniel Stewart and then Mike Kelly."

"Who both were victims of earlier drive-by shootings."

"Yes, but we don't know if these crimes are connected."

Jennifer sighed. "Inspector...."

"Jennifer, we know the facts of last night's abductions from our preliminary investigations, but any links to past crimes requires further investigation by us."

"And the abduction of Sophie Weaver?" Jennifer then asked.

"Again we need to investigate if that's connected."

"Sophie Weaver's family was questioned by your detectives after those drive-by shootings."

"That line of investigation didn't find a connection to the drive-by shootings or evidence of illegal activities."

"Thank you Inspector; I'll be in touch."

"You're coming here?" Inspector Rogers asked.

"Yes."

"Please keep to the facts as we know them."

"Facts are facts and hypothesis is hypothesis."

"Alright Jennifer."

"Thank you Inspector."

Jennifer ended her call to turn her chair.

"Mick, Fergus?" she called across the newsroom.

"We're ready to go when you are," Fergus said.

Jennifer stood. "Well then, let's go!"

She followed Mick and Fergus to the carpark for what was now becoming a major story, state-wide. With luck this might give Jennifer her career break. She didn't want to leave Orange, it was a great place to live, but if she stayed eventually Prime will close their newsroom like other networks had already. On that basis these shootings and abductions in normally sleepy Young were like a late Christmas present. Jennifer climbed in front, Fergus got behind the wheel and Mick got in the back, for what was becoming a familiar drive.

* * *

All rostered daytime officers and the two detectives from CIB gathered in the Operations Room where Acting Inspector Rogers had taken over proceedings, not surprisingly. For sure they had a drug war on their hands, and if Acting Inspector Rogers wanted to be promoted beyond acting, he wanted these crimes to be solved.

"Well, Detective-Sergeant McDonald," Inspector Rogers started. "What's your observation about what's going on?"

"Clearly with the daughter of a suspected drug-dealer associated with a bike gang abducted," McDonald began, "followed by two suspected drug-dealers abducted by a bikie gang; these are related."

"Do we know which bikie gang did these abductions?"

"We have witness reports of patches or colours but no positive identification."

235

"We need to know which gang," Inspector Rogers said.

"Aah..."

"How about we show pictures of all known gang colours to witnesses," Luke said.

"Excellent idea!" Inspector Rogers looked around. "Senior Constable Cox and Constable Gill; you can do that. Now the next step. CIB will interview families of the men abducted yesterday evening, while Senior Constable Scott and Constable Hewson will search the house of the bikie-gang drug dealer, and bring all who live there in for questioning."

"Inspector...," McDonald began.

"Scott and Hewson know Bishop, his partner, the local guy who lives there, and they know the house. They're best-placed to do this."

Luke mentally agreed with that.

"Alright, let's do this!" Inspector Rogers said. "We need results!"

Luke headed to their car while thinking. They will search with a warrant if necessary, and might find drugs which could be used as leverage, but it was unlikely Bishop or the others would give-up a bikie gang. That could go seriously wrong for them. The most they could get were charges for trafficable quantities of narcotics which didn't solve their bigger cases: the missing girl, Sophie Weaver, and the subsequent abductions of Stewart and Kelly.

"You're thinking," Alice said.

"Let's do this search and bring them in for questioning, if they agree. But they won't tell us, will they?"

"No they won't but we have to do this."

They climbed in for the drive to 37 Blackett Street where Luke with Alice by his side, knocked on the door. Jack Bishop in shorts and thongs answered.

"Senior Constable Scott of Young Police, with Constable Hewson as you will remember. Do you mind if we search your home or do we need a warrant?"

"Search away," Jack Bishop said with a sweep of his hand.

That meant if there were once drugs there they were now gone. Either they knew of the kidnappings before they happened or perhaps they heard it on the news.

"Be careful of their belongings," Luke whispered to Alice.

"Like last time," Alice replied.

"Yeah."

They searched including roof cavity and garage, but found no drugs or anything out of the ordinary. Luke gathered Jack Bishop, Jessica Weaver and Josh Ward in their living room.

"Do you all mind coming to Young Police Station for questioning," Luke asked.

"I'm getting tired of this," Jessica Weaver snapped.

"This is something easily resolved just by doing it," Luke said.

"I understand. Can you give us a taxi voucher to get home?"

Not unreasonable. "You'll get a taxi voucher."

"Then we're yours."

## Chapter Thirty Three

Josh sat in the same interview room: waiting, waiting, waiting. The door opened for Senior Constable Hewson and Constable Scott to enter.

"Ah, my turn to be interrogated," Josh said.

"Don't be a smart-arse, Josh," Senior Constable Hewson said before sitting beside his female colleague. "We want to ask you some questions on the record, and you're entitled to have a lawyer present if you so desire. If you can't afford a lawyer, one will be appointed free of charge to you. Do you understand?"

"I understand and I don't need a lawyer," Josh said. After being interviewed before he knew he had that option, but he knew he would be fine, he hoped. The only evidence they had was the note from Daniel which Jessica burned after they heard the news that morning. Senior Constable Hewson then pressed the two keys on that old tape recorder.

"Senior Constable Luke Scott and Constable Alice Hewson interviewing Joshua Ward," he said. "What can you tell us about the abductions of Daniel Stewart and Mike Kelly last night?"

"What I heard on ABC radio this morning."

"Do you know who's involved with the abductions of Daniel Stewart and Mike Kelly?"

"No I don't." Josh sat up straight. "You can ask me that question a hundred times and my answer will be the same."

"Your girlfriend, Sophie Weaver, seems to have gone missing."

"She has and I'm worried about her, but like the abductions of Daniel Stewart and Mike Kelly, I don't know what's happened to her. If I did I would get her back!"

"We have a record of a phone call from Trevor Davies of Devil's Ride Motorcycle Gang to Jack Bishop, yesterday evening."

"You'll have to ask Jack about that." Josh had an idea. "With Sophie missing the last thing I want is bikies abducting people."

"What if Trevor Davies suspects Stewart or Kelly of abducting Sophie Weaver?"

"Do you have evidence of that?"

"We're asking the questions."

Josh nodded while thinking that was 'no'.

"Is there anything else Senior Constable Hewson and Constable Scott, or can I go now?"

Senior Constable Hewson pressed another key on the tape recorder. "You're free to go, Joshua Ward."

Josh left while hoping Trev was able to extract what happened to Sophie from Daniel Stewart, soon.

* * *

Luke reported to Inspector Rogers.

"What did you find, Senior-Constable?" he asked.

"Like last time their house was clean, and neither Bishop, Weaver or Ward admitted to anything, as you would expect with a bikie gang involved."

"Yes, right. Well we identified the Devil's Ride gang being involved with these abductions. What do you know about the two abducted men: Stewart and Kelly? Who supplies them?"

"Rumoured to be supplied by Franco Romano of the Griffith Mafia, who's based in Wagga."

"Local mafia kidnapping Weaver's daughter seems possible," Inspector Rogers said.

"It does, Inspector." Luke thought, and with CIB not around he had a chance to guide this investigation. "Should we ask our colleagues at Campbelltown CIB to investigate Devil's Ride, and at the same time our colleagues in Wagga Wagga CIB to investigate Franco Romano?"

"Coordinated raids to release all hostages?"

"Yes."

"Good idea Senior Constable. I'll tell Detective-Sergeant McDonald so we're on the same page, and then get this underway."

Inspector Rogers walked off to do something worthwhile.

"McDonald's going to be really pissed-off with you," Alice whispered.

"Let him be pissed-off," Luke whispered back. "What matters is rescuing Weaver, Stewart and Kelly. Surely this is our best option for that."

"I'm glad I'm not Campbelltown raiding a bikie gang headquarters!" Alice then exclaimed.

That was for sure. Franco Romano would roll over easily enough but a bikie gang! Armed to the teeth: handguns, rifles, shotguns: they would need their Tactical Operations Unit and even then it wouldn't be easy. But still it had to be done.

* * *

Jessica sat in an armchair to light a cigarette. Normally she didn't smoke much but these past days had changed that.

"What did you tell them about that phone call from Trev?" Josh asked Jack.

"Trev is an old friend from Wagga, which he is, and he rang to offer commiserations about the disappearance of Sophie who he knows. They asked me if Trevor Davies would have been behind these abductions, but I told them you would have to ask him that."

"Will the police question Trev?"

"I hope not," Jessica said.

"The rule is we don't give him up and he doesn't give us up," Jack said. "If the police raid Devil's Ride and take Daniel Stewart into custody, then they'll find Sophie instead of Trev finding her."

"Yeah, alright.  I just want my girl safe and sound."

Jack went to Jessica to put his arm around her shoulder.

"We all want Sophie back here safe and sound."

Jessica half-smiled.

# Chapter Thirty Four

Jennifer stood behind Fergus, looking over his shoulder as he ran the latest edit through. Good, no excellent in fact. She heard the door to the editing suite open and smelled Tamara's sickly sweet perfume.

"How is it now?" Tamara asked.

"Four thirty-two, just as you wanted," Jennifer said. "It's good."

"Fergus: get that to the control room for the midday bulletin. Jennifer there's a possible development. Campbelltown Tactical Operations Unit raided a local motorcycle gang there, Devil's Ride. There are reports of a number of Devil's Ride members taken into custody, one civilian casualty and one civilian freed unharmed. This might be a coincidence but is worth checking out."

Jennifer understood. "I'll ring my contact at Young Police."

At her cubicle Jennifer scrolled her contacts before making a call.

"Leon Fowler," he answered.

"Leon; Jennifer. We heard something happened at Campbelltown which might not be a coincidence."

"Just hang on a sec." Jennifer pictured Leon finding somewhere discreet. "I'm here Jennifer and you're not wrong. We connected Devil's Ride some time ago and thought there was a strong possibility before further evidence

244

was uncovered.  We forwarded what we knew to Campbelltown CIB who forwarded it to their Tactical Operations Unit.  Unfortunately it went a bit tits-up; Mike Kelly was freed while Daniel Stewart was taken to Campbelltown Hospital in a critical condition."

"What's his injury?"

"Don't broadcast this but he was shot in the head.  He's undergone an operation and now is in intensive care."

"Alright.  Thanks Leon."

"Say hello to Jake for me."

"I will.  See you."

She ended the call then thought.  She scrolled her contacts again and pressed to call.  This time it rang for a quite a while.

"Inspector Rogers, Miss Davies."

"I'm sure you're busy so I won't keep you longer than necessary.  I have a report that Devil's Ride motorcycle gang in Campbelltown was raided, with Mike Kelly freed and Daniel Stewart in a critical condition in Campbelltown Hospital.  Could you confirm this please?"

A moments silence while she pictured the inspector contemplating where that came from.  In fact from her husband's cousin.

"That sums it up," he said.

"Will you be questioning Mike Kelly?"

"He's being questioned in Campbelltown as were speaking."

"Anything else?"

"That's all I can tell you, Jennifer."

"Thank you Inspector Rogers."

Jennifer ended the call. *Yes!*

"Was it connected?" Tamara asked from behind.

"It was. Given this is important I'll write a script now, and take Mick and Fergus to film in front of Young Police Station."

"Good idea. This will go state-wide again."

Jennifer knew that as she turned to type a brief script outlining the facts now confirmed through official channels, but omitting the extent of Daniel Stewart's injury, no doubt for the benefit of family yet to be informed. Jennifer wondered what, if anything, this had to do with the missing schoolgirl and decided to put that in the end. *'One question that remains unanswered is the fate of missing Young High School student, Sophie Weaver, abducted on her way to school, and whether her disappearance is related to this drug war currently playing out in the normally quiet inland town of Young'.* Jennifer read that back, pleased.

"Mike, Fergus?" she called.

"Don't tell me Young again!" and Fergus laughed.

Jennifer laughed too. "I won't tell you but it's Young again."

"This is better than local flower shows and the other exciting stories we usually cover," Mike said.

Jennifer stood. "Let's go boys."

She followed them to the carpark.

* * *

They gathered in the Operations Room with CIB sidelined for Inspector Rogers to now run this investigation.

"I'll brief all involved officers as to the current state of play," he began. "As you know Campbelltown Tactical Response Unit raided Devil's Ride headquarters where Mike Kelly was released, but unfortunately Daniel Stewart was injured and is now in a coma. Franco Romano didn't have Sophie Weaver at his home and he refused to speak with Wagga Wagga CIB, while Mike Kelly refused to speak with speak with Campbelltown CIB. The fate of Sophie Weaver remains unresolved. Does anyone want to comment?"

"I'm sure Luke Scott wants to comment," Detective-Sergeant McDonald said.

Eyes turned to Luke who had to say something. "Either Stewart, Kelly or Romano is hiding Sophie Weaver, probably under the care of third party," he said.

"Fair comment," Inspector Rogers said. "Uniform must be over their shift times so you can clock-off. CIB remains on duty until we work out a strategy."

Luke and Alice headed to the locker room.

"McDonald's mightily pissed-off," Alice said.

"Tell someone who cares," Luke said. "Mafia have a sort-of code of behaviour where if they kidnapped a girl and it

247

went bad like this, they'd give her up. Stewart and Kelly aren't mafia so now I'm inclined towards those two."

"To cut our options for investigation down?"

"Kelly seems straight-up, like the new guy Bishop's straight-up in a way. Let's look at Stewart, I think. First his partner, then relatives and then friends who might be helping." Luke thought. "Tomorrow, unofficially."

"Yeah, alright."

"She's a missing sixteen year old girl," Luke emphasised.

"You're right."

Luke thought only a person without a moral compass would kidnap the 16 year old step-daughter of a rival. Luke felt somewhat short of breath; they didn't have too many options to find Sophie Weaver. Her life literally hung in the balance, more and more as each day passed.

* * *

Sophie heard the crunch of tyres and the rattle of a diesel engine. She knew who it was. Dressed the same, different shirt maybe, carrying a pizza box with a roll of toilet paper under his arm. He put them down to unlock the gate and enter the cave. Sophie stood to accept both, wordlessly.

"I need more water," she said.

He walked to the ute parked only a couple of metres away, to grab a bottle. Sophie put the toilet paper down to take that bottle, unscrew the top and pull out the stopper. She drank – so thirsty. Drank and drank. Then she opened the pizza box:

ham and pineapple. She ate a slice – half cold but like yesterday quite tasty. Gourmet pizza.

"Are you alright?" he said.

"You know my name," Sophie said.

"Are you alright, Sophie?"

"I'm not dying but the sooner I get out of here, the better."

"I was told this is only for a few days."

"Even a few days is too much." Sophie ate another slice. "Every day you're more involved," she said but his weathered face remained unmoved. Country people, especially farmers, were like that. Stoic.

"If there's nothing else I'll leave you to it."

"Yeah, whatever," Sophie said as he locked the gate before walking to his ute. She sat cross-legged on the cold, cave floor to eat the last of her pizza before it got stone cold.

## Chapter Thirty Five

Prime Evening News was at six, where once more they gathered in the living room. Josh wasn't surprised that one of the lead stories was the ongoing drug war in the small, inland town of Young, but he was surprised when the detailed story came on, to see Jennifer Davies in front of Young Police Station telling viewers that police had raided the Devil's Ride bikie gang in Sydney, taken a number of members into custody, released one hostage, Mike Kelly from Young, who was helping with enquiries, while Daniel Stewart from Young was in intensive care in a critical condition.

Jessica grabbed the remote to turn the television off but for once didn't light a cigarette. "Now what?" she asked.

Josh had an idea. "I say we pay Lisa Fox a visit to see if she can help us. Be nice, I don't think she's involved and Daniel's in trouble too, but we're in trouble and we need her help."

"Do you know her?" Jessica asked.

"Yeah, I do."

"You do the talking. Actually, do you need us to be there?"

"Let's not overwhelm Lisa," Josh said.

"Let's go," Jack said. "You drive, Josh."

Josh knew the way, Jack didn't, and it didn't take long as driving anywhere in Young didn't take long. Josh rang the buzzer for Lisa to ease the door open a fraction, then all the way.

"Hi Lisa," Josh said. "I'm sorry about what happened to Daniel."

"Come in Josh."

Lisa, fastidious in her appearance, was about the same age as Jessica and had a similar, slim build. She invariably wore tight jeans like that evening, coupled with a black silken blouse.

"This was your bikie mates," Lisa said.

"You know it was, but the shooting was probably the police trying to rescue Daniel."

"Great rescue," she said flatly. "I know you want to find Sophie but I can't help you. I told Daniel not to tell me anything, which was a mistake."

"Has he been going out to care for her or anything like that?"

"No, he hasn't."

"Is there anyone you think would be looking after Sophie?"

Lisa tilted her head. "I'll give you his phone; it's got all his contacts. When those bikies took him they left it behind."

Josh followed Lisa to their bedroom, mirrors everywhere, and a black iPhone beside their king-sized bed. Lisa handed it to Josh.

"This might help you," she said.

"Thanks Lisa."

"Good luck Josh."

Josh left for his car where he scrolled Daniel's contacts. Too many but Josh had the answer.

"Do you mind if I call my brother and a friend to help us?" he asked.

"Yes, good idea," Jack said.

Josh pulled his phone out to ring Glen and Emma.

* * *

It was their routine to eat dinner at six before watching the ABC news at seven, and the 7.30 current affairs show after. That evening Sally grilled lamb chops with vegetables and potato. Frank should have enjoyed his meal but his mind was in a cave not so far away.

"You seemed distracted," Sally observed.

It was impossible to hide feelings from a wife of 35 years. Frank couldn't talk about the girl in the cave but he could talk about another and bigger problem outside.

"That rain was useful: topped up the tank for the house and even part-filled our dams. Already there's green but no feed."

"A green drought," Sally said as an observation.

That's what farmers called paddocks that had one or two centimetres of growth. A sea of green but not enough to feed their valuable breeding stock; let alone thinking about restocking.

"Unless there's good follow-up rain, we'll have to keep buying fodder."

"Daniel's been good lending us money."

But at a price worse than paying interest. Frank ate the rest of his meal in silence. Later, Sally washed their plates and Frank dried. Then to the living room of their old homestead. Built by Frank's grandparents with brick walls about a foot thick covered in cement render painted white, and a veranda around the perimeter. Shaded and insulated, even on the hottest day it was cool inside, and on the coldest day easy to keep warm. They lit the old kitchen stove, fed it with firewood from fallen gum tree branches, and that was almost good enough to heat the entire house and brew tea too. Winter evenings they ran an electric bar heater in the living room for a few hours.

Their living room echoed with memories of past generations, but with Daniel moving to Young, Frank would be the last Stewart to live there. That was a shame, and a bigger shame that Daniel made his living from doing questionable things, and none more questionable than kidnapping a schoolgirl from Young, reported every day for the past few days. Sally switched their television on; Frank sat in a big, old, leather armchair, draped with a cloth cover as was always the way, to watch ABC news.

The introduction covered Corona-virus in China, whatever that was but now spreading to Italy, and a bikie gang raid in Sydney.

After the Corona-virus story which seemed serious, the bikie gang raid was yet another chapter in the war against drugs, given these bikies, in this case the Devil's Ride gang, made their money from drugs, like Daniel. Apparently Devil's ride kidnapped two suspected drug-dealers from Young, which pricked Frank's interest. In an attempt by police to release these hostages, one was shot and now was in a critical condition in the intensive care unit of Campbelltown Hospital. That more than pricked Frank's interest.

"I have to go for a moment," he said, to leave Sally and sit at the kitchen table. There he found his contact for Lisa.

"Hello Lisa," Frank greeted.

"Hi Frank and I know why you're calling. Daniel is the hostage in a critical condition."

"How?" Frank gasped.

"He kidnapped that girl that's gone missing and bikies took him away because of that. Then police got involved but they fucked-up."

"I'm sorry about this, Lisa."

"I'm sorry for you, Frank. When I hear something about Daniel's condition, I'll call you."

"Thanks Lisa, bye."

"Bye Frank."

Frank then contemplated his old Nokia mobile while thinking, thinking, thinking. He was an accomplice to kidnapping that girl; in fact she threatened Frank and she was a feisty bitch too. For sure she would cause trouble. Frank sighed then realised this was Daniel's problem so Daniel had to fix it when he recovered. Frank wasn't going to jail simply for keeping his breeding stock alive during the worst drought of all times. He was a farmer, Daniel was a criminal who kidnapped schoolgirls, and Daniel would have to deal with this girl when he could.

"Are you alright, Frank?" Sally asked.

"That suspected drug dealer that was shot is Daniel."

Sally gasped and put her hand to her mouth.

"They said suspected drug dealer but they got that wrong," Frank said, "but they didn't get the shot part wrong."

"I'll ring the hospital now."

Sally used their landline to call directory assistance, then Campbelltown Hospital, where she found Daniel was in a coma in intensive care and not seeing visitors.

"We'll have to wait until Lisa tells us when he's recovered," Frank said.

"I wish I could see him but we'll have to do that."

In the meantime that girl Sophie would have to stay in that cave.

* * *

255

Most of the contacts on Daniel's phone were first name only but at least many had addresses. Their plan was to take four Young-based contacts each and knock on doors, plead for Sophie while saying they wouldn't tell the police or anyone else, and the first to find Sophie would ring everyone else. If not, gather at Blackett Avenue to plan their next steps. Jack got the Charger out with Jessica riding along. Josh went from household to household to household, being both polite yet firm as he asked questions they rehearsed as a group. If you've been helping Daniel by looking after Sophie, tell me where she is and this will go no further. As long as Sophie is home safe, what happened these past few days will be forgotten. Sympathy expressed about Sophie's plight and helping if they could, made Josh sure the guys he visited weren't involved. Eventually he returned to Blackett Avenue to see Glen and Emma's cars. Shortly after, the Charger eased into the garage.

Jack and Jessica came into the living room and didn't have to say they didn't find Sophie. Glen hadn't, Emma hadn't and Josh hadn't. By then it was almost 11.

"We need to ring his contacts who don't have an address," Jessica said. "I'll do that tomorrow morning."

Josh scrolled Daniel's contacts again.

"I have classes tomorrow morning," Glen said. "I can help in the afternoon."

"I'm free all day," Emma said.

"Emma; can you and Jack cover addresses in Cowra?" Josh asked. "I'll do Canowindra. I'm interested in 'Mum and Dad' listed in his contacts, and Amy Stewart who must be a relative. Perhaps even his sister."

"These people might be at work during the day," Emma said.

True. "Well, if we can't do this face to face to face, we'll ring them."

"If we can't ring them we'll visit again in the evening," Glen said. "I can help with that."

With that they broke up for Josh to go to his room, he was sure to have another restless night of little sleep.

## Chapter Thirty Six

Canowindra was a slow-moving village just north of Cowra, known for museums, galleries, classy cafes and hot air balloon rides. Amy Stewart lived in a renovated early 20th Century house near the centre of town, in white-painted concrete over brick and surrounded by a veranda; looking fresh like it was built yesterday. The garden was gorgeous, more like a park than a yard, as were many gardens in that part of Canowindra. Josh pulled a white cord on a brass bell beside the front door, for it to clang noisily. Moments later the door opened to reveal a freckled redhead, maybe in her 30s, with a toddler at her feet.

"Amy Stewart?" Josh asked.

"I'm Amy Stewart and this is John," she said while glancing down at the little boy.

"Hi Amy; I'm Josh Ward from Young. I'm sorry to hear about Daniel but there's a bit of a story about him. Daniel kidnapped Sophie Weaver from Young, and that's why he was taken hostage by that bikie gang and later shot when police raided that gang."

"Pardon?"

"Daniel is a drug dealer involved with kidnapping schoolgirls and staged drive-by shootings."

"That can't be right."

"Young is like here where people know what's going on," Josh said while thinking Amy Stewart didn't know about

258

Daniel so wasn't involved with the kidnapping of Sophie. But he was there so he might as well ask. "Do you have any idea where Daniel has kept the missing schoolgirl from Young, Sophie Weaver, or have you been looking after Sophie for Daniel? If you have and you tell me, we'll take Sophie home and not tell anyone about your involvement."

"I don't know what you're talking about but this doesn't seem like Daniel to me."

Josh was annoyed by her smugness. "Daniel lives in an expensive new house, he has it full of expensive furniture, and he drives an SUV that cost almost as much as your house here. Yet, he doesn't seem to work. That doesn't make sense unless he's doing something illegal like dealing drugs."

"I'm insulted by your accusations and I want you to leave."

"You can be insulted and I can leave, but that's what he does. That doesn't matter to me; what matters is finding Sophie Weaver."

"I want you to go now."

"I'll go, but think about Daniel's finances."

She slammed the door while Josh was certain Amy Stewart didn't know anything about Daniel, drugs or Sophie. He went to his car to switch the GPS back on. He typed the address, waited for it to calculate; then set off for a 10 minute drive. As was the case with country roads, 125 O'Briens Road actually meant 1.25 kilometres from the highway, where Daniel turned onto the driveway for a farm with an old house a hundred metres further along, while surrounded by paddocks green with no feed. Behind the old house was a yard with a few sheds both new and old. Josh parked on the drive that ran alongside the house to that yard, to walk to the front door and use a knocker.

A deep, rough voice called: "Can I help you?"

Josh turned to see a farmer right down to his Akubra hat, had come from the yard at the back to stand next to Josh's muddy car. Josh went to him.

"Are you the father of Daniel Stewart?" Josh asked.

"I'm Frank Stewart, Daniel's father."

"Hi Frank; I'm Josh Ward from Young. I'm sorry to hear about your son Daniel but there's more to that story. Daniel kidnapped Sophie Weaver from Young, and that's why he was taken hostage by that bikie gang and later shot when police raided that gang."

Frank crossed his arms but said nothing, which seemed wrong. Josh continued.

"Do you have any idea where Daniel has taken Sophie Weaver, or have you been looking after her for Daniel? If you have and you tell me, we'll take Sophie home and not tell anyone about your involvement."

Again silence while Josh tried to understand that stern face but there was nothing at all.

"I can't help you with any of this, so you should go," Frank Stewart eventually said.

One last chance. "We're not interested in anyone who's been helping Daniel; we just want Sophie Weaver."

"Can't help you."

"Alright," Josh said while sensing Frank knew something. "I'll go. Can I give you my number so if you find Sophie Weaver, you can call me?"

"Just go, Josh."

"Alright."

Josh got into his car, backed a little way before turning to head back to Canowindra to visit the last two contacts on Daniel's phone. Josh knew they would be a waste of time. This man, Frank Stewart, knew and he might be looking after Sophie. Frank wasn't surprised by Josh accusing Daniel of kidnapping and he didn't deny being involved. Almost for sure Frank was involved. Josh turned onto the highway while wondering how to find out.

Josh drove to the house of the next contact, Jake in Canowindra, which was locked with nobody home. Josh rang Jake who worked at the BP garage so Josh drove there. Josh ran through his story, Jake offered 'sorry mate, can't help, don't know, that doesn't sound like Daniel', which seemed genuine. The next was Mick who again wasn't home, but Josh caught up with Mick at PJ's Woodfired Pizza on the crooked main street, which had a menu quite unlike anything Josh had seen before. Josh was told that didn't seem like Daniel and Mick hadn't seen or heard from Daniel in yonks anyway, but would Josh like a pizza? Josh did where Mick recommended supreme pepperoni which had mushrooms, onions, green capsicum and mozzarella. Josh ordered that and a flat white, and while he waited for his meal he thought. Those sheds on Frank Stewart's farm looked irresistible. Not in broad daylight though. It was starting to get dark by seven but not totally dark, so Josh would return then. Josh decided to drive to Cowra, which had a larger population than Young and many more services and attractions. He would visit the Japanese Gardens; perhaps even find out why Cowra had Japanese Gardens, before returning to Frank Stewart's farm closer to seven.

* * *

Luke got in early to clear things with Leon before logging into COPS to search Daniel Stewarts record, where Stewart was arrested but not charged for low-level drug possession in Canowindra in 2003. That gave his date of birth and his address then, and helpfully his parent's names and addresses, being the same address. Luke jotted parent and address details into his notebook before searching for the electoral division of Canowindra, which was Calare with the office based in Orange. He wrote the address and telephone number.

Luke rang the electoral office for Calare, gave his identification and asked for a search of the electoral rolls, which was refused as he expected. If all else failed they would drive to Orange to search the electoral roll in person, as was allowed.  Alice hovered.

"Alice," Luke said, "Leon gave us the all-clear to search for Sophie."

"Now he'll have to deal with CIB if we find her."

"The most important thing is finding her."

"Agreed.  Let's go – where?"

"Lisa Fox."

After a short drive, Luke pressed the buzzer of 18 Matthew Street: an immense and expensive house totally lacking charm.  He heard a woman shouting at a child or children before the door opened to reveal a slim, 30-something woman, dressed like she was going to a party in the tightest of designer jeans, a silk blouse, full makeup including lipstick and eye shadow, and her blonde hair styled. Not what Luke expected for the partner of a patient in critical care.

"I'm not speaking to you!" she exclaimed and slammed the door.

"Lisa!" Luke shouted.  "I just want to find the girl."

The door opened again.  "Can't help you," she said. "Don't know a thing and that's the truth."

Luke suspected that was the truth.  "What about family or friends looking after her?"

"Don't know.  Mike was his closest friend but you lot have him."

"Family?"

"Perhaps. His parents live on a farm near Canowindra and his prissy sister lives in town there."

"Do you know her name?"

"Amy Stewart."

Luke pulled out a card which Lisa took. "For Sophie Weaver's sake, if you think of anything, please call us."

A pause. "Yeah, alright."

Lisa slammed the door.

"To Canowindra?" Alice asked.

"Let's go."

Luke checked his notebook before programming the address into their car's GPS navigation system. It didn't take long before they turned onto a rough, farm driveway with the house dead ahead. It was a house that would have driven Chloe ecstatic, given its age and originality. Luke pulled up just off the driveway to walk with Alice to the front door. Luke used an old, brass knocker; original like everything else. Frank Stewart was old, creased, tanned when Luke showed his warrant card.

"Frank Stewart; I'm Senior Constable Luke Scott of Young, and with me is Constable Alice Hewson. I would like to ask you a few questions."

Silence, and it was silence out there except for the warbling of magpies. "Alright," Frank Stewart said while Alice had her notebook ready.

"Are you the father of Daniel Stewart?"

"I am."

"Do you know of the whereabouts of missing Young schoolgirl, Sophie Weaver?"

Silence for a moment. "I've seen stories about her on the news but I don't where she is."

"Are you sure."

"I can't help you."

Luke sensed something wrong with Frank Stewart's vacant look. He didn't know what it was but something was wrong. But short of arresting Frank Stewart on a vague suspicion, Luke didn't have a choice. He gave a card to Frank Stewart.

"If you come across Sophie Weaver, please call us at Young."

He didn't acknowledge that.

"Thank you Mr Stewart," Luke said.

The door closed. Luke walked with Alice to their car.

"He didn't ask why you asked those questions or seemed surprised in any way," Alice said.

That was true.

"I don't trust him," Alice then said.

"I don't trust him either but we can't arrest him on that." Luke thought. "I won't bother with the sister; we'll head back to Young to talk with Leon."

"Yeah."

Luke climbed into their car, waited for Alice, and then drove away.

* * *

Josh parked his car behind a gum tree in O'Briens Road before stepping across an animal grid between brick posts to enter Frank Stewart's farm. There Josh spread wires on an internal fence next to the drive; unlike the boundary fence this wasn't barbed, to cross paddocks towards the house but at a distance. Heading almost due east Josh passed the house to now advance on the yard. There he spread another internal fence to enter the dirt yard with two big sheds of farm machinery, some of which was ancient and belonged in a museum like a cart that once would have been pulled by bullocks, and some was modern and shining especially a big green and yellow tractor. One older building, a large, lightly rusted corrugated iron shed, was the most likely. At a corrugated iron door secured by a chain but not locked, Josh paused and looked around to spot nothing moving. He unhooked the chain, tried to pull the door open but it had sagged and dug into firm dirt, so Josh lifted as he opened it to enter cool semi-darkness. Inside was totally amazing: built from round, rough-hewn posts and smaller, rough-hewn round frame members, literally tree trunks and branches cut more than 100 years ago, and an earth floor packed early last century or even earlier. It was like a museum with horse harnesses hanging from hooks, a rough timber bench covered in rusting tools, even a blacksmiths forge with more rusting tools, but no sign of Sophie. Josh spotted a corrugated iron partition to his left so he went there. Inside the partition was quite dark; Josh wished he had a torch. Then Josh heard something moving. Josh eased deeper into that partitioned area.

"Sophie?" Josh asked quietly as his eyes slowly became used to darkness. "Sophie?"

"What are you doing here?" a familiar deep, rough voice asked.

A sharp pain on Josh's head. He felt his legs go weak, he crumpled, and then nothing.

# Chapter Thirty Seven

Josh felt dizzy and uncoordinated. It was uncomfortable where he lay and quite cool too.

"You're awake," Josh heard from a familiar, sweet voice.

"Sophie!" Josh exclaimed.

"Sssh; you were knocked on the head by that guy."

"What guy?" then Josh realised. "Frank Stewart, Daniel Stewart's father."

"So that's who he is," Sophie said.

"At least you're safe but now we're a bit fucked," Josh said. "Daniel's unconscious in hospital so we lost all chance of releasing you through him."

"We are fucked, aren't we?"

"Not totally. I rang Jessica to tell her where I was going."

"Let's hope she can connect Frank to here."

"It's not just Jessica and Jack; Glen and Emma are helping."

"That guy Frank doesn't give anything away."

Josh knew that. "That's why I was rummaging around the sheds at his farm. He must have hit me on the back of my head which really hurts."

"Let me see." Sophie parted Josh's soft curls. "You have a bump but it's not bleeding."

"My head aches worse than a headache, but I'm sure I'll survive."

"That man, Frank, comes every day with food and water," Sophie said.

"I had dinner at Canowindra so I'm fine. Do you sleep on the cave floor?"

"I have to."

"That's awful Sophie."

She shrugged her shoulders, now barely visible as dusk had almost faded to a summer's night.

* * *

Glen rang Josh but it rang out. The next time Glen rang it went straight to voicemail; either in use or switched off. But Josh wouldn't be calling someone else if he saw Glen tried to call. Glen wondered if Josh's exploration had gone to shit. He looked to Jessica.

"No answer," she commented.

"No answer at first, and I think it was then turned off," Glen confirmed.

Jessica lit a cigarette while frowning. "This has gone far enough," she said before drawing on her cigarette. "I'm certain Daniel's father is involved in this. Does anyone disagree?"

Silence.

"Good," Jessica said. "Now we take this to the police and let them handle it. This place is clean, they might have their suspicions about us but they've never been able to find anything. The police believe Sophie was kidnapped by Daniel

269

and we now know his father has done something to Josh." Jessica frowned. "His name's Frank, Josh told us."

"His name's Frank," Glen confirmed, while thinking it was like mother, like daughter. Josh once said whatever Sophie wanted Sophie got, and the same with Jessica. If she wanted police involvement, she got police involvement. But she was right.

"Jack," Jessica said. "Get your Charger out. If Glen and Emma don't mind we'll tell the police. They might take more notice of adults."

"That's fine," Emma said. "I'll go home. I've a few texts to answer, but please let me know the minute you know something. If I don't answer, text me."

"Alright Emma and thank you for your help."

"Thank you for inviting me to help. I hope things turn out well."

"Are you staying Glen?" Jessica asked.

"I'd like to see this through."

"You might as well come with us; you're the brother of your missing brother."

They headed out to a fibro garage like the fibro house, to climb into Jack's pride and joy. Glen had done his research to find there were two versions of the 'six pack' Charger, the E49 with a hotter engine built in limited numbers for race homologation, while the less highly tuned E48 was built in larger numbers. Glen reckoned this was an E48 with stripes to make it a lookalike E49, but still a valuable car. Anyway it was past eight in the evening and dark when they drove to Young Police Station to press a buzzer on the counter, behind which was one-way glass and a brown door. A constable without a name tag emerged without introducing himself. He leaned against the counter.

"My name's Jessica Weaver and I believe we've found my missing daughter Sophie."

"And how did you come to this belief?" was the bored response.

"Sophie's boyfriend Josh Ward visited Frank Stewart, the father of Daniel Stewart who kidnapped Sophie, and now we can't ring Josh."

"So the battery on his phone is flat. Where is Frank Stewart?"

"He lives on a farm at 125 O'Briens Road, near Canowindra."

"Alright," the constable said as he pulled a pad and pen from beneath the counter to start writing. Then he spun the pad around and gave the pen to Jessica.

"Read that and sign it, and I'll give it to the Duty Sergeant.

"Will you do something?" Jessica asked.

"We'll see what we can do."

Jessica grimaced while signing, after which the constable tore the signed witness report page from the pad, before taking it through the door.

"They're not going to do anything," Jessica grumbled.

"It's late at night," Frank said.

"Yeah, I suppose so." She frowned. "I think those two constables who searched our house those times, Scott and Hewson, are the most switched-on here. If we tell them our story they might put the pieces together and actually do something."

Frank rubbed his chin. "I reckon you're right," he eventually said.

"Do you have any ideas, Glen?"

Glen did. "Do you know either of their first names," he said as he pulled his phone out. He didn't use Facebook, mostly Instagram, but he had a Facebook account and these guys might be on it. Most likely they were.

"What was his name Frank?" Jessica asked. "I know, Luke Scott."

Glen typed that in, and Young. "Found him," he said. "I'll send him a Facebook message to call you. What's your number?"

"0416 998 312."

Glen typed that. "I wrote: you know where Sophie is and to call you straight away."

"Thanks Glen," Jessica said. "We'll go home now."

They got into the orange Charger for the drive to Blackett Avenue. There Glen really should go home, he felt like he was intruding, but he asked Jessica and Jack to call him as soon as they knew something, which they promised to do.

* * *

Despite summer and a mild evening outside, it was cold in that cave. Poor Sophie had been stuck there for too long. Josh and Sophie cuddled to keep warm: he wore jeans and a t-shirt while Sophie was in her summer slacks and her white blouse. Josh knew he wasn't going to sleep.

# Chapter Thirty Eight

Luke picked up his phone to notice a Facebook message from Glen Ward. He pressed it to see a message to call Jessica Weaver on 0416 998 312. Odd, no, not expected. Luke memorised the number to dial. It rang a few moments.

"Hello," Jessica Weaver greeted.

"Hello Jessica, this is Senior Constable Scott. What can I do for you?"

"I'll make this as simple as possible. Lisa gave us Daniel's phone and we've been talking with all his contacts. Yesterday Josh went to see Daniel's father Frank Stewart near Canowindra, where Josh thought Frank was involved with Sophie's abduction. Josh planned to go back to Frank's farm and that's the last we heard from him. We tried to call Josh but his phone is switched off."

"Doing your own policing is dangerous, Jessica."

"Yeah, I know; but it was either that or leave Jessica to the fate of you guys. I think you're alright but the rest...."

Luke agreed with that observation. "What's done is done," he said. "I'm heading into the station soon. I'll check with the shift sergeant but I'm sure my partner and I can take a drive to Canowindra."

"Not just a drive, this is serious!"

Jessica Weaver was right. This was too much of a coincidence, especially after their suspicions about Frank Stewart yesterday. "I'll do whatever it takes."

274

"Can you ring me when you find something?"

Not unreasonable for a mother. "I'll be in touch."

"Thank you."

Luke ended that call and headed to shower, while Chloe was up and making breakfast. After his shower and shave, Luke walked to the kitchen deep in thought.

"Is there trouble?" Chloe asked.

"I might have a lead on that missing schoolgirl," Luke said. "Strictly speaking I should hand this to our detectives, but to make things happen I'll look into it with Alice."

Luke ate his muesli, drank his filtered coffee; before heading to work. Changed and suited-up, he went to Leon in the Operations Room.

"Something's on your mind," Leon said.

"Jessica Weaver rang me at home," Luke said. "Josh Ward was investigating Frank Stewart and now Josh has gone missing. I'd like to take Alice to check this out."

"If you find something, you and I will get into trouble," he said.

"Like yesterday, to find Sophie Weaver is more important."

"Yeah, alright."

"Thanks Leon. Alice?" Luke asked.

"Ready when you are," she replied cheerfully.

"We're paying a visit on Frank Stewart."

"I don't trust him."

"You and I both."

* * *

Yet again Frank parked outside of PJ's Woodfired Pizza. He knew young people liked pizza and it didn't hurt to give the girl, and now that boy, food they liked. Frank strolled inside where the young man behind the counter, Mick, looked rather bored.

"Another takeaway pizza, mate?" he said.

"Yeah," Frank said, "for two friends staying with us. Just give me something you think is nice."

"Supreme Pepperoni?"

"Alright."

Mike wrote a docket, tore it from the pad and stuck it under a clip above the counter which opened through to the kitchen. The cook in white pulled the docket from the clip, browsed it, and set to his task.

"Rain's been good," Mick said.

Frank nodded his head. "It seems like farmers always complain but we need good follow-up rain to make a difference."

"My old man's a farmer so I know what you mean."

"What does he graze?"

"Cattle."

"Sheep on my place although we've largely destocked."

"The old man too."

"Money for fodder for the stock you've got left then becomes a problem."

"That's for sure! The old man must owe as much as his place is worth. I don't know how he's going to pay it back." Mick paused. "It's climate change, you know."

"Greenies got that right."

"Too true, mate."

The cook slid a pizza on a round tray onto the counter. Mick used a spatula to slip the pizza into a box and folded the top.

"That'll be twenty-one dollars."

Frank pressed his card against the terminal and watched for it to be approved.

"Receipt?" Mick asked.

"No, it's fine."

Frank took the box to the ute and soon was on his way to the cave. There he unlocked the gate to carry the box and two bottles of water inside.

"Another pizza!" the girl whined.

"Yeah, well...," Frank said. "I'll get something different next time."

The girl sat cross-legged beside the box while the boy bent down to pick up a slice.

"You know, Frank Stewart, you're now in deep shit," the boy, Josh, said.

"I'm not a criminal, Frank replied automatically.

277

"From where I stand you are. If you call this off now you might get away with a suspended sentence."

"What does that mean?"

"A conviction but no jail time."

"Can you guarantee that?"

"No, but it's more than likely."

"I'm leaving this for Daniel to sort out."

"Daniel's in a critical condition."

"Yeah, I know." Frank wondered. "What do you know about being convicted for dealing drugs?"

"Have you been dealing? No, Daniel. If he's convicted even if he doesn't do time, the worst part of it will be having his assets seized as proceeds of crime. House, car; the lot."

"If he gave money to his family?"

"That will be seized as well."

Frank sighed. This was more than just kidnapping. This was the hard work of four generations of Stewarts wiped off the face of the earth. Frank getting a suspended sentence for looking after the girl and abducting the boy, maybe, but using drug money to run his farm on top of that? Probably not. So jail and Frank didn't want to go to jail. Shame was one thing, locked away was another, but he wasn't a criminal able to defend himself against the types you find in jail. Frank sometimes pictured being stood-over by a group of bikie-type thugs who'd been in and out of jail all of their lives. No, he knew he couldn't deal with that.

"What to do you say, Frank?" the boy asked. "You'll let us go?"

Frank sighed while he thought. "Could you tell people I wasn't involved?" he asked.

"It's too late, Frank," Josh said. "People already know I came to visit you, and others will be asking Sophie what she did these past days. We can't make this go away but we can tell them you treated us decently."

"Yeah, you've been good," the girl said.

But because it was drug money financing his farm he'd lose the lot, so Frank couldn't let them go. Silently he left the cave, locked the chain, got into his ute, reversed it, and headed back to his farm. Headed back to his home.

* * *

Luke turned onto O'Briens Road. Across the grid, along the drive to the house. There Luke knocked on the front door which was answered by a 60's woman, no doubt Sally Stewart.

"Sally Stewart?" Luke asked to be sure.

"I'm Sally Stewart."

"I'm Senior Constable Scott of Young Police, and with me is Constable Hewson," Luke said. "Is Frank Stewart home?"

"Frank's out."

"Do you know when he'll be back?"

"I'm not sure."

Luke had an idea. "Has Frank been going out at the same time most days?"

"He goes out at different times."

"How long does he go out for?"

"Usually an hour or two."

"Thank you."

Luke headed to their car, unfortunately easily spotted. Luke drove it past the house to the yard out back, around in a circle and then alongside the house again, hidden from anyone heading along the driveway but facing to intercept if necessary.

"Now we wait," Luke said while getting out.

"An hour or two," Alice confirmed, as she got out to join Luke.

"I wonder what Frank Stewart could be doing for an hour or two?" Luke asked rhetorically.

"Looking after Sophie Weaver."

"He might have Josh Ward now."

"Ah. They rang you."

"Yeah."

Waited and waited as the radio on his shoulder contacted other units to respond to various trivialities, and those units acknowledged.

"Someone's coming," Alice said.

Luke forgot about his radio to spot an older-style ute turning across the grid. Closing now, probably Frank Stewart. Luke waited, arms crossed, as that older, white ute drew near before turning towards the house, unfortunately,

280

because the driver of that ute now could see their car. There the ute stopped at a distance of about 30 metres. Frank Stewart climbed out holding a rifle!

"Get down!" Luke ordered Alice as he got behind their car for cover. Luke drew his Glock 22 automatic pistol from his thigh holster as Frank Stewart aimed something more deadly than the usual 22 rimfire for shooting rabbits and foxes. It was solid and chunky with a scope.

"He shoots kangaroos with that," Alice said.

That made sense; kangaroos were a pest to farmers too.

"I'll ask him to surrender," Luke said. "Trouble is we can't shoot him, because we'll never find that girl and her boyfriend.'

"Well, ask him."

Luke put his head up to aim his pistol just in case. "Frank Stewart, we just want to talk with you. Put your rifle down and lay face down, hands behind your head."

Luke watched Frank Stewart aim, and ducked as Stewart's rifle discharged with the crack echoing around the farm. Now what? On his vest Luke had a taser and capsicum spray, while at his waist he had an extendable baton. Of his non-lethal weapons, the taser had a range of 10 metres, the spray three to four metres, and the baton no more than a metre. None were good enough to deal with a rifle. Ideally Luke should have been wearing body, armour except that was in the boot of the car and he would be shot before he got it out.

Luke pondered radioing for help but other officers coming onto the scene might put Frank at risk, and therefore the girl at risk, so he decided not – yet.

Luke put his head up to aim.

"Frank Stewart!" Luke called. "We just want to talk."

"You're not putting me in jail and taking my farm."

"I'm just interested in Sophie Weaver and Josh Ward, that's all. Please tell us where they are."

Again Frank Stewart shot his rifle just as Luke ducked his head. Luke decided to try once more. He put his head up.

"You can't shoot at us forever, especially if we call backup. Be sensible."

Frank Stewart had his telescopic sight aimed at Luke who thought to stare him down, except Stewart shot again. Luke dropped down as a bullet passed through the car centimetres close. *Fuck!*

"You should radio for backup," Alice said.

"Yeah, well, the radio's not working." Luke thought. "Can you keep him engaged but not kill him while I cross to his ute. If I can get behind it, I'll be in range to taser or spray him."

"Fuck Luke!"

"The girl's life depends on it."

"And her boyfriend."

"Him too."

"Alright. Be careful!"

Luke took a big breath before sprinting to the nearest poplar tree for cover, now a few metres closer. Another big breath: the next tree, and the next tree, and the next tree to reach the closest tree but one to the ute. But when Luke moved, Frank Stewart shot at him. Alice then shot her pistol to which Frank Stewart aimed and shot towards. In the midst of that, Luke ran to the closest tree to the ute. Now he needed covering fire. Mentally he willed Alice to take a few more shots, which by magic she did. Great! Head down Luke ran to the back of the ute, to dive face-first onto soft dirt. On knees and elbows Luke crawled as Alice took a few more shots with Stewart responding. Closer and closer as Luke removed the taser from his vest. There he stopped to look around a rear wheel; close but dangerous. Lying full-length Luke aimed the taser when Frank hesitated from returning fire to Alice, and immediately spun around just as Luke pulled his trigger. With a look of shock Frank dropped his rifle and cried out before he crumpled to the ground, when Luke released the electric charges. Luke sensed someone moving to grab his pistol and aim.

"Hang on!" Alice exclaimed as she picked up Frank's rifle.

"Sorry," Luke said. "Is Frank out of it?"

Alice threw Frank Stewart's rifle away before dropping to her knees.

"Frank Stewart, where's Sophie Weaver and her boyfriend Josh Ward?" Alice asked.

Stewart lay still and silent.

"Frank, answer me!" Alice shouted while shaking Frank. "He's out." Alice pressed her radio. "Young 313."

"Go ahead."

"Code India, 125 O'Briens Road, Canowindra. Suspect tasered, ambulance requested."

"Ambulance being despatched."

"Acknowledged."

*Now what?* Luke had an idea. He hammered on the front door of the house for Sally Stewart to ease it open a crack.

"It's alright Mrs Stewart," Luke said. "Your husband has been tasered and is semi-conscious. An ambulance is on its way."

"Why?"

"Because he shot at us.'

"Why did he do that?"

Luke decided to lie. "I believe Frank Stewart is involved in something serious. Now Mrs Stewart, you can help him. Do you know of any sheds or outbuildings or anything like that, away from this farm but not too far away, that your son Daniel might be familiar with?"

"What's this about?"

"This will help your husband."

"Well, there's a cave that Daniel and Amy, my daughter, used to play in, but it's locked these days."

"Can you show me this cave?"

"What about Frank?"

"Constable Hewson will stay with Frank and escort him to hospital."

"You say this will help Frank?" she then asked.

Luke could only continue his lie. "Yes it will."

"I'll show you the way to the cave."

Luke guided Mrs Stewart to Alice standing over Frank Stewart lying still on the ground.

"Mrs Stewart is showing me to a cave where we'll probably find what we're after," Luke said.

"Alright."

They got into the car.

"Drive to the highway and turn left," Sally Stewart said.

Luke did.

"Now, first on the right."

Luke turned onto a dirt road somewhat rougher than O'Briens Road.

"Just along here."

Luke drove carefully on firm dirt with many exposed rocks.

"Just here."

Luke rounded a curve past a large boulder to see a cave, including a gate padlocked with a chain.

"Stay here," Luke instructed Sally Stewart, before running to the gate to be face to face with Sophie Weaver and Josh Ward.

"Glad to see you," Sophie Weaver said.

"Are you alright?" Luke asked.

"I'm fine."

"Does Frank Stewart have a key?"

"He does."

Luke thought then pressed his radio.

"Young 313."

"Go ahead."

"Request Constable Hewson search Frank Stewart for keys."

"Acknowledged," was Alice's voice. "Keys found."

"On my way," Luke said.

"Acknowledged," Alice replied.

Luke let his radio go. "I'll get keys from my colleague to get you out of here."

"Acknowledged," Sophie Weaver said and laughed.

Luke knew Sophie Weaver wasn't too bad but she needed observation, as did Josh Ward. Luke got into his car.

"What's this about?" Sally Stewart asked.

"Your son Daniel kidnapped the missing schoolgirl, Sophie Weaver, while your husband Frank has been looking after her here. I'm assuming Frank kidnapped Sophie Weaver's boyfriend, Josh Ward."

"Why?"

"Because Daniel Stewart is a drug-dealer and Sophie Weaver's step-father is also a drug-dealer."

"Pardon? No, that can't be right."

"It is right, Mrs Stewart."

Luke started his car to return to the Stewart farm. When he turned onto the highway he passed an ambulance, lights flashing but no siren, heading towards Cowra. At the farm, Alice waited.

"I have Frank Stewart's keys," Alice said. "Cowra will have officers meet that ambulance and guard Frank Ward in hospital. I suppose we'll have to charge him in Cowra."

That was rather complicated. Young detectives would be massively pissed-off that Luke didn't get them involved, while Cowra would be massively pissed-off that an arrest was made by Young police officers on their patch. Lurking was Sally Stewart, who Luke didn't sympathise with. He wondered how a woman could allow these crimes to happen without being suspicious.

"You can go now, Mrs Stewart," Luke said. "Make sure you don't leave the vicinity of this farm so you can be interviewed in due course."

Sally Stewart meandered towards her house while Luke thought her unsteady walking was shock.

"Let's go Alice," Luke said.

Not long after, Luke unlocked the padlock on the chain to the cave. Sophie Weaver emerged with Josh Ward.

"You two need to go to hospital," Luke said.

"Ooooh!" Sophie Weaver whined.

287

"Just for observation. I'll tell your mother Jessica. Do you have anyone I need to tell, Josh?"

"Just tell Jessica," Josh Ward said.

Luke hypothesised Josh Ward came from a broken home, not uncommon, but still broken. Perhaps Sophie Weaver became his safe haven. In any case Luke radioed for an ambulance to be sent to the GPS location of his car. When that was acknowledged he heard Sophie Weaver laugh.

# Chapter Thirty Nine

Josh woke, didn't know what time, but the ward was dark yet far from quiet as noise came from the nurses' station quite close.

"Josh?" Sophie called from the next bed.

"Yes Sophie."

"Thanks for rescuing me."

"Jessica really rescued us."

"That's right. I can't wait to get home to our nice bed."

That narrow, hard, hospital bed was only marginally better than sleeping on the floor of the cave. Josh couldn't wait to get home; 37 Blackett Avenue was his home now.

Lights flickered on just before the rattle of a trolley. Trays of food were handed to all patients: cornflakes, a container of milk, cold toast, a small pat of wrapped margarine, a small container of orange marmalade, and fruit juice. Lovely – not. Josh was hungry and ate the lot while Sophie picked at it.

Not long after breakfast, Jack and Jessica visited. Josh and Sophie were free to go. First Jack would take Josh to pick up his car before they drove home. Josh followed the Charger all the way to Young to park his old and faded car in the street. Old and faded it might have been but it got him around and it was reliable. Heavy on petrol though.

Inside Sophie made coffee. She gave Josh a mug before they assembled in the living room.

"Frank Stewart was arrested and is being interviewed today," Jessica said. "Daniel Stewart will be charged when, or if, he recovers. For us, I've decided with Trev now remanded in custody, to change our income earning strategy here in Young. What do you recommend, Josh?"

"There aren't many worthwhile jobs here," Josh said. "Small businesses can be profitable, though. If you can find a business where the owner's selling and get the books checked out by an expert, that's your best option."

"Are you still planning to move to Wagga?"

"We'll move by semester one next year, to pay board to Sophie's father's parents. We'll probably have to stay in Wagga after our studies given there are few decent jobs here."

"You'll only be an hour and a half away," Jessica said. "We'll look for a business that will suit us. You mentioned gardening, Josh. I can't imagine too many people in Young paying for gardeners."

"There are big blocks on the outskirts with totally incredible gardens. I'm sure those who provide gardening services have that wrapped up, but if one is selling you could buy his business, which is really buying his clients."

"We'll look into that," Jessica said. "I think we can do gardening."

"If you want to rent a better house I can ask my grandfather to find you one."

"Thanks Josh, we'll do that.  Alright, what are you two going to do now, or do I have to ask?"

"Mum!" Sophie exclaimed.

"You're only young once."

"It's not only the young," Jack said, which Jessica ignored.

"We'll go to our room now," Sophie said.

Inside with door closed, Sophie sat on their bed.  Josh sat beside her.  There he took Sophie in his arms, something they did in the cave to keep warm.  That morning on their bed it was different.  Love.

* * *

With Sophie abducted it hadn't been right for Glen to attempt to rekindle his relationship with Lucy.  With Sophie now safe it was a good time but Glen couldn't bring himself to ring Lucy like that.  Yet he knew if he didn't contact Lucy, nothing would happen.  Face to face he stood a better chance of avoiding total rejection.  A few days after that decision, Mum and Kev had a big drinking session followed a big argument.  Glen just had to get out the house for a few hours. It wasn't late so he drove to Lucy's house to press the buzzer beside the front door.  Mrs Ryan answered.  After greetings she promised to get Lucy.  It took some time which wasn't good news, but eventually Mrs Ryan escorted Lucy to the front door where she greeted Glen with a shy 'hi'.

"Can we talk?" Glen asked.

"Alright.  Come inside."

They went to her mostly pink bedroom where Lucy shut the door. Glen had rehearsed this. "Things happened which changed things, but I hope only temporarily," he said. "I like you Lucy and I'd to start again with you."

She looked through Glen towards the door behind him. "Now that I've had time to think, school this year is going to take all of my time."

"Are you sure?"

"I'm sure."

"Could we see each other after your exams?"

"That's a long time away."

"By then you won't be busy while other things will have died down."

"That's true."

"Is that a maybe?"

"Yeah, maybe."

Glen sensed that really was no because if Lucy was at all keen she would have agreed before Glen found someone else. Glen liked Lucy, she was pretty and friendly with a well-hidden sexy side, even if that caused a problem. Now there wasn't much Glen could do.

"Good luck with your exams," Glen said. "Maybe I'll see you when you're free."

"See you Glen."

Glen left feeling down. It was a shame they just had one weekend together. He might contact Lucy after her exams if he was still free, but for now he would respect her request.

Anything else would be harassment.

# Chapter Forty

The next big downpour was Thursday the fifth of March, the heaviest so far. That rain, on top of February's rain, meant there was a chance of crops and grazing, and even a return to prosperity, in inland New South Wales. Maybe Young would emerge from economic crisis, but even if it did Young would never be totally well-off; more like getting by. Josh was sure, no certain, that as much as he liked Young he had to move on, as he turned into the carpark of the Chinese Gardens, as usual for a Saturday. There they were. James was a nice guy, couldn't do enough for his friends, but a geek who endlessly played games and spent a lot of time on the internet. That far from wasted as James now had a decent job at Propellerhead IT. Matt was addicted to base, as was Leah his girlfriend. They showed the signs: acne, pimples, scarred lips and rotting teeth, and being perpetually a bit out of it, but harmlessly. Alana boasted about her older boyfriend Mike who seemed to beat her, given she'd walked into a few doors or fallen down a few stairs. Justin was a totally nice guy, while his fiance Toby moved to cosmopolitan Young from Grenfell to the north. Josh knew Toby's sexuality would have been a problem in Grenfell but not in Young, which was bigger and more grown-up that way. Noah was getting by on part-time work at Ambos Stockfeeds, with the delightful Charlotte as his girlfriend. Charlotte had a decent full-time job in a winery out of town. Lucas: overweight on too much takeaway and too much coke, the drink, had Zoe who was seriously overweight to make a matching pair. Zoe had traded sex for affection for as long as Josh could remember, until she hooked Lucas into a relationship. Next was Emma who set her own path in life and was happy with her choices. The last was Glen who said he gave Lucy time before contacting her, but Lucy didn't want to date him for now. Josh thought a bit of persistence on Glen's part, not harassment but more of an attempt, might have rekindled a relationship that initially showed good promise. But Josh couldn't live his brother's life for him.

There they were: the class of Young High School, 2017; now in early 2020.

"Hi all," Josh said, echoed by Sophie before they sat. The good: James, Charlotte, Emma, Justin, and Toby as an honorary member. The bad: Matt, Leah and Alana. The in-between: Noah, Lucas, Zoe and Glen. Josh knew he would miss them all when the time came to leave.

"What do you all think?" Josh asked for no particular reason.

"Well," James said, "this corona-virus seems serious. We might even get locked-down like in other countries."

"Do you think so?" Emma asked.

"It's possible."

"That won't do my business any good," and Emma laughed.

"What do you actually do, Emma?" Justin asked.

"I work for myself," Emma said.

"Doing what?"

"Working."

Josh knew Justin wasn't going to get more out of Emma than that, although he'd heard on the grapevine that James, who was financially settled, visited Emma when she worked as Lucy. The Lucy's of this world relied on geeks and the unsuccessful in love like Glen.

"I don't know what work you do, Emma," Justin said, "but any of us who face customers will be hit hard by a lockdown. Worse that we're casual and we don't have paid leave."

"I face customers and that's a problem for me," Emma said. "You and Toby work in a cafe."

"If we're locked down we won't be able to pay our share of rent and food."

"Who else?"

"Me," Charlotte said. "I sell at Chalkers Crossing winery."

"Me at Mitre 10," Josh said while looking around. "All of us, except Glen and Sophie studying."

"Corona-virus is the last thing we need," Emma said.

Too true.

# Epilogue

Josh had never thought teaching would be so hard as he sat beside Sophie working through her next module. In particular teaching took patience. Nonetheless they were making steady progress when he sensed Jessica enter the dining room. She sat at the table while Sophie typed on Josh's laptop. Sophie stopped and put her head up.

"Don't let me stop you," Jessica said.

"I've finished this module," Sophie replied.

"Josh, I don't know what I would have done without you," Jessica said. "I never went far at school as you know. Sophie said you could help with her assignments but we never expected a pandemic lockdown and online learning! Do you two want lunch? Ham and salad rolls?"

"Just salad in my roll, Mum."

"Me too," Josh said.

"Won't be a minute."

Jessica didn't take long where, with the laptop pushed to one side, they ate.

"I wanted to get out so I bought these rolls and some milk," Jessica said. "At least I can do that."

"Why didn't you go far at school, Mum?" Sophie asked.

"This is a bit of a story but there's time for this story in a lockdown. My parents tried to be strict on me but I was a bit rebellious, and the stricter they were the more I rebelled. I knew guys were attracted to me, and being me I played along

297

with that. Jason asked me out one Friday night, I think he was 18 or something, and I was 15. I sneaked out of our house for Jason to take me to the pub where he bought me some drinks, mixed sprits. I didn't like those drinks but I drank them anyway; quite a few in fact. I don't remember much after that. The next night Jason then bragged to his mates at the same pub that he took Jessica's cherry, but that was overheard by a police sergeant who knew I was underage. Sergeant McIlroy then came to our house, and what a catastrophe to have the police asking for me! I told him I didn't know because Jason bought me drinks and then I didn't remember. Well, that led to the hotel owner and the guy serving at the bar being interviewed and charged after police looked at the hotel CCTV. By this stage Jessica the drunk slut was all over Leeton. My parents stopped me from going out, everybody called me names; it was quite a thing in place about the same size as here. In the end I decided to leave so I hitchhiked to Wagga. There I went to Centrelink for Newstart but I didn't have a bank account, so I went to the nearest Commonwealth Bank but I didn't have enough ID documents. The teller was nice and told me to wait, and later took me to births, deaths and marriages where I got my birth certificate. I had some money so I stayed overnight in a motel, and the next day I had Newstart. That meant I had to search for work but there weren't many jobs for a 15 year old who'd only completed year 10. I bought a newspaper where there was a room for rent in a share house, and with job hunting and getting my shit together I didn't notice I'd missed a few cycles until the bump started to show. I went to the clinic where I was 12 weeks pregnant. I just couldn't terminate something I could see and feel so I decided not to. Not long after I bumped into the teller from the bank who'd been good to me and he sensed I was upset. He took me to a cafe where I told him my story. That's your dad, Sophie."

"Ah," she said. "I once knew a Jason."

"What was he like?"

"He was my first boyfriend but we didn't last."

"Your first doesn't matter; it's the last who matters."

"I met Josh and we played games, and later we went outside on an evening I'll never forget. I was dying for us to kiss when Josh asked me. He was good with asking. What I don't understand is if I wanted to kiss Josh, why I didn't ask."

"A girl who asks for kisses and more is a slut," Jessica said.

"Of course. In school these days we're taught about respect which Josh followed to the letter," Sophie said. "I admired that."

"Women are men's equals and entitled to their personal spaces," Josh said. "I've never met a woman who wasn't equal to any given man, so that's why I always follow what we were taught."

"We'll be equal together forever. I'll pass this year, I suppose, but I'm not sure what comes after."

"This lockdown won't last forever and then life goes on," Josh said. "I think your hairdressing might work but I'm not sure about studying business. People always need haircuts and hairstyling, but some or maybe many businesses will go out of business now that they're closed, which might be a problem."

"You don't want to be on Newstart which doesn't pay enough," Jessica said, "and you don't want to be forced to look for jobs that don't exist. That's terrible."

"If I don't think studying business is a good idea I'll think of something else." Josh thought. "We're the generation worse off than those that came before us, even before this pandemic."

"You are, sorry to say, because I love you both."

Josh thought Sophie's hairdressing certificate most likely would get her a job of some type, and if he picked a different career to study, probably healthcare like Emma, he would get a job in that too. Now that corona-virus had come out of nowhere they would remain the generation worse off than generations that came before.